MIDNIGHT LOVERS

by

CHARLES NUETZEL

WRITING AS "STU RIVERS"

The Borgo Press
An Imprint of Wildside Press

MMVII

Contents

Introduction

The jazz world has always fascinated me, and in recent years I have been really enjoying a rather interesting experience: swing dancing every week with a big live band supplying the music (seventeen top-flight musicians who have been in the business all their lives, having worked with all the major big bands in their youth—and continue to make great music in their elder years). It has been neat getting to know these men on a personal level. Their stories many times reflect my own experiences as a young man nosing around in the show-biz field.

While these musicians are all quite dedicated and serious about their music, and many happily married, there are some who "don't have a life" outside of the music. It can be a tough world to survive in, and many of their friends have been dragged down by drugs and booze. Others have been highly successful and are now rich in their semi-retirement. Music still is their center, the dedication, and their passion. Otherwise why would they still be blowin' like crazy?

I mention the above only to illustrate a point: the following story (as well with my *Blues for a Dead Lover*) offer up a true sense of how it is for many people in show-business.

This is a story of a musician struggling to make

it at the beginning of his career. It tells what it is like to take a gig in a small town, and how, well....

Glenn Fletcher had worked hard to make it in the jazz world, where casual relationship had been an ideal way to survive loneliness—and Ivy Turner, the combo's singer, served up "night lunches" after the last set.

For Glen the music was everything until he met Lynn Bennings. Then things changed at light speed! Sparks flew both ways. If it wasn't love at first sight it was dangerously close.

Lynn loved jazz, and for some time she had had a secret crush on Glen. In fact, she arranged for his combo to be signed up at the local night club in the small town her father just about owned.

And big trouble followed, for Mr. Earl Bennings would do anything to protect his daughter from fortune hunters. This was a man nobody dared to cross—for his reputation threatened deathly violence!

—CHARLES NUETZEL
Thousand Oaks, California
July 2006

Chapter One

The red-haired girl closed and locked the dressing room door, turned and faced Glen Fletcher.

"Okay, Ivy, what's it this time?" Glen demanded, finding it hard to keep his eyes off her wonderfully voluptuous figure. The green dress accented every sexy curve, cut deep at the neckline to reveal two large thrusting breasts. Ivy Turner grinned seductively, her light green eyes sparkled.

"What you think, lover-boy?" she inquired, stepping forward in a rolling-hipped fashion that made her large breasts tremble against the tight fitting, deep neck lined dress.

"Oh, come on, Ivy...we don't have time for anything like that!" Glen cried, running large fingers through his short-cropped blond hair.

"Fifteen minutes is long enough for me," Ivy laughed, coming to a stop in front of him. Her breasts just touched his chest. Her eyes flared hot. "I need it, Glen. You know that. You know how I am."

Her hips surged against his and rubbed back and forth.

The expression on Ivy's face was wanton heat.

"Come on, *please*!" She pleaded with her eyes, lips all but touching his, breasts yielding and supple

7

where they pressed to him. He knew Ivy didn't wear a bra under the stage gown. She had told him many times it wasn't necessary to wear a bra. How right the woman was. Her plump breasts were kept in excellent condition by daily exercise. They were firm and fully packed, self-supporting.

"Please, we don't have much time!" she urged, sliding a hand around his neck in a thrillingly caressing motion. "You know how it is with me!"

"Sure, you need it like a hole in the head!" Glen laughed. They had screwed around a lot in the last months since Ivy had joined his combo. It had started the first day they met, when she'd come in for an interview. She wore a low cut sweater, casual looking, but the buttons on top unlatched to show off her breasts to a very nice advantage. It was sex at first sight as far as he was concerned; and she liked being with a man late at night—or any time of day!

Since then it was a fairly casual thing; if she needed it she'd come to him like this. Or when they were finished for the night and could go back to the hotel or motel where they'd have a "night-lunch" as she called it. Ivy had a good imagination and served up with some delectable dishes.

"Come on, lover," Ivy breathed against his lips. Then her tongue ran along the surface of his mouth, tingling the nerves.

The first time they had played around the fact that each wanted to leap into bed with the other; it had taken a full day to get to a bedroom. The interview first, then the audition, dinner and later, after the club had closed, a night lunch at Ivy's apartment, which led to the more intimate relationship

8

that had continued ever since.

Glen didn't fight any longer. It was useless to fight Ivy once she'd turned on the raw sex like that. They wouldn't even need fifteen minutes—and didn't have that much left.

They were between sets, and it was possible to keep the customers happy with silence and booze for only so long.

Ivy pulled up her dress, gathering the skirt around waist.

"See? No panties!" she announced in glee. She was five feet six inches of hot, passionate sex, offering itself for quick, frantic tumble.

Ivy knew the road to fast sex; she knew Glen well enough to drive his need to the point of no return. Her hands moved over him, playing hot teasing games until he felt the need burst full bloom.

There had been no lingering build up; no real foreplay.

He could feel the pressure building within himself; and then she suddenly moved, swift, skillfully, not waiting. Her whole body enveloped him.

"You're so good!" she sobbed, clutching to him.

And now their climax was slashing into reality.

All at once she strained, trembling all over and then held him tightly in place.

A sob uttered from Ivy's lips as a pleased:

"Oh, it was great. How I needed it!"

Regardless of how great it had been, Glen felt a distant annoyance with himself. The passion moved him into action and then afterwards he a sense of emptiness, as sense that a very important emotional element was always missing.

This feeling had been a personal hell ever since

his first and only true romance—almost five years ago. That was with Carol Smith. She had played him for a complete sucker. But at the same time had made it possible to discover what it was like to be in love—even if it was a one way thing.

She hadn't let him bed down with her until their tenth or so date. They'd gone to a motel and after turning out the lights undressed and climbed into bed. "It was a beautiful necklace you gave me!" she said, coming into his arms, gently allowing the natural build-up to flare their passions. Then she had murmured in pleasure, saying how wonderful he felt. Afterwards she claimed she was seldom intimate when men. But that he was special. The way she devoured him with her lips was sure evidence that either she had a great imagination or a hell of a lot of experience. Only later he learned she bedded almost every guy she dated and was highly oral.

She had seen the necklace in a jewelry store window and hinted her desire for it. The damned thing cost over a hundred dollars. Because of that they had celebrated and ended up at the motel. The next date he'd figured she would sleep with him, but found an excuse. Not until he had given her another expensive present was she willing to go to a motel. Her love-making was great; but nothing more than high-class prostitution. Later he learned she was having an affair with an older man—whom she finally married. The guy was rich as hell.

At first Glen had gone on a drunken binge, and then later sought out everything with skirts on.

The trouble was, Glen realized, that a jazz trumpet player never had a chance to stay in one place long enough to really develop a prolonged romance.

10

And the women he met in the business were too concerned about their own bloody careers to be interested in anything of a serious nature.

Ivy had fit in that last category.

The rest were just ladies who offered themselves up to the "celeb" on stage. There were always groupies willing to sleep with musicians.

"Well, love," Ivy said, "Gig-time!"

Hal Kenyon, the bass man, knocked on the door, called: "You guys ready?"

The mockery in the man's voice assured Glen that he knew exactly what had been going on.

Cursing under his breath, Glen winked at Ivy. "Okay, Hal. Get the boys on stage!"

They were in the middle of *What Is This Thing Called Love* when the *Stage Door Club* manager, Henry Jones, came up to the bandstand. He motioned to Glen.

"A woman wants to see you after the set," the man said.

"Which one?"

"Table Nine."

Glen looked across the small night club, through the crowded dance floor. It was a moment before he could see Table Nine, which was to the far left of the bandstand. He got a short glimpse of an attractive, well-dressed young woman. She had dark black hair that flowed over creamy shoulders. During the next few minutes he kept looking in her direction, trying to get a better look at the woman.

Ivy came up to the mike on cue for her solo and nudged him slightly. "No hanky-panky, Glen-boy!" she murmured softly, giving him a frozen smile.

Glen turned, faced the four musicians on the

stand behind the mike. Placing the golden trumpet to his lips he softly blew a background riff that led into Ivy's solo.

As Ivy sang out the chorus to *What Is This Thing Called Love,* Glen turned, looking at her neatly packed fanny that pushed out against the back of her tight dress.

Then his eyes wandered across the dance floor toward Table Nine.

This time he got a better view of the woman. She looked about twenty-two or twenty-three.

There was a lovely, innocent expression in her eyes and her delicately featured face broke into a winning, attractive smile as their eyes met.

Glen nodded and then returned his attention to the music lilting out of his horn.

The next few numbers seemed to take forever. Their sets were a little over forty minutes long, and he had gotten the message from the woman at Table Nine halfway through the set.

There had been a lot of girls, women and matrons, who were fascinated by a jazz musician. They numbered with the towns through which combos made their endless flight for fame. He had met enough, ended in the rack with many.

It was so damned easy to get some female companion that sometimes Glen wondered what was happening to the human race.

Now the more he looked at the woman at Table Nine, the more convinced Glen was that she was something different. It was partly in the way she was dressed. Expensive. Maybe it was his immediate mood. He didn't know. But the minutes dragged hellishly, painfully slow.

What did she want? The usual? He wondered, intrigued. Every time he looked in her direction there was a warm smile to meet him.

Was she out for a thrill? A night of excitement?

Finally the set came to an end and he put the trumpet to his lips for the last time, leading the group into *A Foggy Day,* the fast walk-off theme.

As the dancers returned to their tables and the musicians got up to leave the stage, Ivy slipped up beside Glen. Her face was molded in lines of jealousy.

"Glen...you wouldn't!" she said in a pleading voice. "That fifteen-minute kick wasn't enough. I need a real party tonight."

Glen laughed, patted her arm and looked down her neckline. "Ivy—you know the business. I have to consider the group's interest. If—"

"If you are called to do things beyond the call of duty—you jump at the chance," she laughed harshly. "Okay—you play your little games—but don't expect me to be hanging around, a-panting. I got my pride, too, love."

With that, Ivy twisted around and left the stage.

Chapter Two

Glen moved down to the dance floor and walked toward Table Nine. As he came to a stop before the dark-haired female, Glen smiled and said:

"Well, I understand that you wanted to see me, Miss …"

"Miss Bennings. Lynn," she said in a low, husky voice. "Please do sit down. Can I buy you a drink?"

"Thanks!" Glen sat, looked at the woman.

She was even lovelier close up. Her nose was pert, upswept slightly, giving her a cute facial expression. Her eyes were large, dark-brown, and as they met his he felt an inner tingle shoot, through him, starting from the base of his spine and rushing up to his neck.

The waiter came to the table and Lynn Bennings said: "Another Scotch and soda for myself and for Mr. Fletcher—" She turned, questioned him with her eyes.

"Beer."

"Won't you have something more…?"

"No, not during working hours. Once I tried that, on the invitation of a young woman—and I didn't blow much music that night." Glen tried to laugh, but it came out embarrassed sounding.

The waiter left and they were silent for a moment.

Glen had a chance to examine the woman more closely.

Her neckline was much higher than he might have liked, but the shoulder straps fell down around her arms, revealing beautiful darkly tanned flesh. Her breasts looked well-formed and created excited images in his mind.

"You find me attractive?" she inquired in a soft, almost embarrassed voice.

"I'm sorry...I didn't mean to stare."

"Well, at least...well, I guess it's good to have a man look at you that way." Silence, then: "I've enjoyed your playing quite a lot."

"Thanks."

The drinks came then. She took her Scotch and soda, raised it, and waited for him to pick up his beer. She tapped his glass and for a moment their eyes met.

In that moment Glen felt a strange sensation move over him. It was as if he were suddenly one with this Lynn Bennings: as if they were magically connected both body and soul. He felt her emotions reaching out to embrace him, tenderly revealing all there was of her.

Shaking his head, Glen took a sip of the beer and looked away across the smoke-filled night club.

Abruptly he felt nervous, out of sorts, unsure of himself. Much like a school kid who is in the presence of a young girl he has a crush on.

He turned and looked at her again. His eyes followed the line of her dimpled full-red lips, her shallow cheeks, down to her white throat, and lower to

16

the thrust of her dress.

What a neat, beautiful package, he thought. Yet, for all her immediate control of the situation, there was a child-like innocence to her eyes; a delicate helplessness that seemed lost.

She turned her eyes again to his and that emotion reached out, embraced him. Like a little wounded doe, a frightened little child who hides, runs, refuses to show itself to the world. Then a veil slowly lowered, like a curtain coming down, and an amused smile moved her lips, dimpling her cheeks, revealing even, beautiful ivory teeth.

"I guess you're wondering why I asked you to come over here," she suggested in her low, bedroom voice. At the beginning Glen had believed the low quality in her voice must have been put on for his sake. Now he realized it was her natural way of speaking.

"I was wondering," he admitted, after taking another good swallow of the beer.

"Well, I guess you don't know much about my family, being that you're just passing through, so to speak. But the Bennings have money and position in this town..." She broke off, looked down at her delicate, slender fingers. "I'm sorry, that sounds snobbish. I didn't mean it that way. Just that I didn't want you to think I'm some sort of kook." Her eyes met his once more. "What I wanted was to hire you Sunday afternoon—your group we don't need the singer, just the combo, and—well, we're giving a party for my mother. It's her birthday and I wanted to have some live music, if you know what I mean. Well, in any case...what would it cost?"

Glen felt the bottom drop out. Up to that moment he had believed she was actually interested in him personally. The blow was crushing. For the first time Glen realized that he was more than casually attracted to her. It was more than mere sex—like so many other women had been. He didn't believe in love at first sight, but Lynn Bennings had hit him in a strange startling way.

He sat there staring at her, unable to believe the impact the woman had on him. It didn't seem possible. He literally felt shaky.

Yet, right from the moment that the manager had come up and told him that a woman wanted to see him, he'd assumed it would be the same old pitch. And all this time sitting next to her he'd been sure there was something in her mind other than a mere business offer.

Well, he told himself silently, *so much for ego-boo.* Not all women are helpless before the winning charm of Glen Fletcher.

"Mr. Fletcher, we will make it worth your while," Lynn told him softly.

"Better see my agent. Monica Hall takes care of bookings," Glen announced sharply.

Lynn blinked and then lowered her eyes to the glass in her hands. "I didn't mean..." There was a short silence, then she asked: "You can make it?"

Glen nodded. "There isn't any booking for Sunday that I know of. I'll give you Monica's number. You can make the arrangements with her." Glen pulled a wallet from his pocket and then got out one of Monica's cards.

Standing, Glen said: "I have to make a living now. I hope we'll see each other Sunday."

"At three in the afternoon. The manager can tell

you where." With that Lynn stood and walked hurriedly away, crossing the room in a jerky, almost angry stride.

Glen stared after her, puzzled. There had been anger and a light suggestion of hurt to her last words.

Had she actually meant something more than a business offer? Was she as disappointed as himself?

He wondered.

Finally Glen turned and walked to the bandstand. A few moments later the group was behind him, getting ready for the first number.

Ivy stepped to Glen's side and asked, "Well, what happened?"

"A gig for Sunday," he answered, fingering his trumpet

"Oh, no! I'd planned on a relaxing afternoon and—"

"You can still have it. She didn't want a singer. Just the group," Glen announced, strangely pleased by the fact.

Ivy's eyes grew wide, her mouth opened as if to say something and then snapped closed. After a few deep breaths she said: "Well that little..." The last word was so muffled that Glen couldn't hear it, but he guessed her meaning from the jealous flare in her light-green eyes.

As he put the trumpet to his lips a glow of excitement flushed over him.

Maybe this Lynn Bennings would turn out to be something special after all. It took a woman to see through another woman's sly attempts at flirtation. Maybe he had something really to look forward to.

Then Glen felt a stab of guilt.

Miss Lynn Bennings was such an innocent-looking woman. He couldn't help believing she needed protection more than misuse.

During the rest of the evening Glen found it impossible to think about anything other than Lynn Bennings. And the more he thought, the more impossible his thoughts became.

There was something about that her that had reached him; really dug deep—and he didn't like that at all!

After the last set Ivy slipped close to him and said, "How about it, love?"

For a moment he didn't even know what she was talking about. Then he saw the look in her eyes.

"A night-lunch?" she suggested. "A personalized dessert, afterwards?" Her smile both mocked and invited him.

Off to Bangsville again, he thought, vaguely annoyed while at the same time excited.

Well, it was better than being by himself, Glen realized, putting his trumpet away.

Night-lunch with Ivy was a full course meal. It was something Glen needed in a physical way. And Ivy was the kind of hot broad willing to dish it out fast, wild and generous.

The minute they got to his hotel room, Ivy was in his arms, thigh pressing against his groin.

"Oh, I've needed this," Ivy moaned in his ear, her breasts heaving against him.

He tried to laugh lightly. Somehow it all seemed meaningless in a way. It was as if this scene had been played out a thousand times with women like Ivy—and they all seemed faceless.

Ivy grinned, moistened her lips with the tip of

her tongue. Her eyes flashed teasingly.

Every movement of her mouth as she sang a song was like some intimate promise. When she was like this, alone with a man, it was and intimate act.

As the dress peeled down her body, then slipped over the curve of her hips, dropping to the floor, Ivy unlatched her bra and those lovely, self-supporting breasts burst free, their nipples already taut and eager for a man's kisses.

"Aren't you going to get undressed?" she inquired.

"I'll fix some drinks. How about it?"

"Great!"

Ivy was now pulling her black lace panties down and he watched a moment as the mouth of her womanhood revealed itself boldly to him. She leaned over and slipped the panties over sensually shaped thighs, then stepped out of them.

Glen then turned and went to the nightstand where a half empty bottle of whiskey stood. Opening it he moved to where two glasses were waiting on the small hotel desk, and started pouring the drinks.

He had half filled the second glass when Ivy came up behind him and slipped her hands round his body.

"Oh, you are hot," she breathed pressing against him.

As he turned, the glasses in each hand, Ivy moved up against him.

"Put those silly drinks down. I want another kind of liquor, first!" she announced.

When her hands had opened his shirt, she moved back slightly slid her lips against his naked hairy chest and tongued him erotically, moaning in delight.

Slowly her lips moved down until they were on the flat of his stomach.

"Hell, Ivy, I can't take that much!" he objected.

"If you'll put those drinks down!" she offered, "we can…make love."

Somehow he managed to get rid of the glasses and their lips fused in deep tongue kisses.

It was like being taken by a wild beast. It was orgiastic and savage and animal. A full course of erotic sensual rape but who was doing the raping would have been difficult to tell. Then he felt Ivy convulsively strain to him.

They didn't move for some time but when he did finally lift away, Ivy was at him like a hungry little bitch in heat.

He rolled over on his back only to have Ivy voluptuously attack him with her lips.

Glen could see it would be a long night and he was glad because it wouldn't be possible to think about anything other than what was taking place at any given moment.

Later would be time enough to think.

The next morning he discovered the untouched drinks upon getting up from bed. Ivy was lying on top of the covers, still naked.

He tiredly stepped into the bathroom and then turned on the shower.

As he stepped into the shower stall the bathroom door opened and Ivy joined him with a little giggle.

"Are you kidding?" he cried in partial horror. "Didn't you get enough last night?"

"Don't tell me *you* got enough!"

He would rather have been alone. But already her actions were causing a very normal reaction within his body and he knew just how useless it was to even attempt to ignore her.

Was it always going to be like this? he wondered.

MIDNIGHT LOVERS, BY CHARLES NUETZEL

Chapter Three

Glen walked down the expansive hallway following the Bennings' butler who had answered the door. There was already a party atmosphere, even though the guests hadn't arrived as yet.

The Bennings' home was on a hilltop that overlooked Davis City like a king on a throne. It was a large, two-story white building with a big roomy entranceway.

The butler turned and walked through a double door. In a stiff, cultured voice he said, "In here, Mr. Fletcher."

Glen entered the small room that was lined with bookcases filled to the brim with endless volumes. A comfortable, well-used desk centered in the room, and a large, heavy man was seated behind it like a lump of fat.

The man's face slowly wrinkled up in an automatic smile. It was the gray-blue eyes that seemed chilled and careful.

The butler said, "Mr. Bennings, this is Glen Fletcher, the musician your daughter hired for today." With that the butler turned and closed the doors after him as he left the room.

Mr. Earl Bennings slowly and laboriously stood

up placing beefy hands on the desk before him and raising his weight upwards.

"I want to thank you, Mr. Fletcher, for coming a little early at my daughter's request. I know you must be a busy man—and realize you no doubt have things to get organized for your duties this afternoon, so I'll make this as short as possible." The man moved thick fingers over the bald spot on his head. His grin widened as he slowly stepped forward and reached out a large hand to Glen.

"Tell me something about yourself, boy," Bennings commanded like a general talking to some underling.

Glen couldn't make up his mind if he liked Earl Bennings or not. He had heard sonic stories about the man since the other night when Lynn Bennings had asked him to play for her mother's birthday party.

Earl Bennings almost owned Davis City. He controlled the papers and owned the city bank, along with a lot of surrounding lands. The police department jumped at his command, as did most of the people in the town. According to rumor he had made at least some of his money during the Twenties by importing illegal liquor into the country. Beyond that Glen knew little about the man.

"Well, boy, I asked you a question!" Bennings announced, cutting into Glen's thoughts.

"I'm sorry. What do you want to know?"

"Just a general outline."

"Why?"

"I have my reasons!"

"I don't think it's any affair of yours, and—"

"Please, do me the honor. I believe I've started

out a little badly. You would do me a great service by having a drink with me." Bennings' eyes grew larger and his features lined again. The large man moved to a cabinet behind his desk and pulled out a bottle of Scotch whiskey and two glasses. "Straight or on the rocks—with or without soda?"

"Any way you like it."

"Maybe you think I'm a queer one. I don't know what you've heard about me—but that's not important." He was silent while pouring two healthy shots of whiskey. He turned, walked to Glen, handed over one glass. "Well, bottoms up!"

Bennings downed the drink in two large swallows.

Glen sipped his carefully. The Scotch was smooth, soothing, and expensive.

"Now, boy, just because I'm interested, how about a little background? I like to be able to tell the guests something about the men...well, celebrities. You know how it is." There was something in the older man's eyes and voice that seemed to make a lie out of his last statement.

Glen considered for a moment and decided it didn't really make much difference.

"There's very little to tell. I've been playing trumpet for almost as long as I can remember. Through high school, through the army, through college—in that order. I caught the attention of some professionals during college, got a job with a band, worked my way up to lead trumpet, and later formed my own group. We're a full-time combo, which is some kind of record. Having a group that stays together, travels across country, and all that. We like one another; respect each other's musicianship. Means a lot. And so we've managed to get to the point where we can almost read each other's minds…musically, that is. My agent is now trying to get a recording contract for us with one of the top jazz labels, and it's just a matter of time before we hit the top." Glen broke off there, suddenly feeling like an egotistical boob. "Well…that's where we're at."

Bennings nodded and then said: "From what I understand, you made quite an impression on my daughter the other night. She's quite a jazz buff. As for myself, well…" He shrugged. "I can take it or leave it—mostly the latter. I'm the old fashioned type. The only Glen I really know much about is Glenn Miller and he was around a long time ago." The man smiled, returned to his small bar cabinet. "Have another?"

"Still have one."

"Well, finish it, boy," the man demanded. "Have another."

"Not before working. I try to remain as sober as possible. A musician who drinks or takes with the needle can't blow straight," Glen explained.

"A lot of the needle work in the business?" Bennings inquired.

"Enough—but not as much as people might think. Most of the guys are hard working; they know their music and their instruments. It's changed a lot since the Twenties," Glen told him, throwing in the last part as a quick ad-lib.

Earl Bennings snapped around, frowned. His thick lips thinned out into hard lines and then relaxed into a grin.

"I used to have a few clubs during the Twenties.

The guys did a lot of things in those days. I didn't think it could change that much in so short a time." He raised his refilled glass to his lips, gulped.

"New generation. In those days most of the guys just blew, knew little about the technical side of the business of music. Nowadays the new generation of musicians study from A to Z...learn the whole bit. There are too many guys who really know their business—you have to be on your toes to compete."

After a long moment of silence, Bennings nodded in reply and said: "Well, I want to thank you for coming in and seeing me, and answering an old man's questions. But—well, I don't get much of a chance to really see and talk to a real live musician, and since I'm paying the bills today I thought it wouldn't hurt to have a little friendly conversation. I really appreciate your coming here today and adding to the over-all atmosphere. We'll want, for the most part, soothing, soft music—background music—but I'll give you ten to one that Lynn has you play a round or two of what she calls 'real music'!" Bennings laughed, moved to the door and opened it. "It's been a pleasure talking to you."

The beefy hand reached out and Glen gripped it again. Their eyes met, almost as if challenging each other.

"If you'll go down the hall to the last doorway to the left, that will lead you into the drawing room. I believe Lynn and Mrs. Bennings are there, waiting for your arrival. They can fill you in on the details...Birthdays! You'd be surprised how much a thing like this will cost a man!" With that, Bennings closed the door behind Glen.

MIDNIGHT LOVERS, BY CHARLES NUETZEL

Chapter Four

As Glen walked down the hall he thought about Earl Bennings and decided that regardless of how he might like or dislike the man, Bennings wasn't the kind of guy to tangle with. There was a tough hardness to this large man that spoke of both success and violence. Bennings was used to getting what he wanted out of life, and Glen guessed he would stop at nothing to have his way.

Shrugging off the thoughts, Glen walked into a nicely furnished large drawing room.

There was a concert grand piano in the far corner, a large marble-faced fireplace opposite the entrance.

He spotted Lynn Bennings sitting on a yellow sofa, a drink in her hand.

She was dressed in a tight red skirt, and white blouse that opened at the front. As he walked into the room her eyes looked up and met his.

For a moment they stared at one another. It was a moment that stretched out to eternity and was over in an instant. All the emotions two people can feel toward each other flashed between them like an electrical storm.

Then the mood sliced away.

How it happened that he even felt such a vivid reaction to a total stranger, Glen couldn't guess. All he knew was that it had come and then faded away as her expression changed. A long moment, when she had been like a little child, reaching out, silently screaming to him like a woman lost; then she became a woman in control of the situation.

She stood. "Mother had to go check on the food...so I'll fill you in on the details."

"I just talked to your father. He says that it has to be background music and…"

"And...you play what you want!" Lynn announced, her eyes narrowing, her voice harsh. "I'm sorry. Just that Dad has old-fashioned ideas. He doesn't even know what kind of music you play. Just play the way you do in the club."

She raised a delicate hand to her loosely flowing black hair, ran her fingers through the fine strands that fell to her shoulders. It was a nervous action. Her eyes were staring into his and the reaching out, the subtle emotional calling was alive in them.

Glen had the impulse to step forward and pull her into his arms.

"Mr. Fletcher—"

"Glen," he offered.

"Glen, you don't know what a thrill this is for me. I've seen you before you came to town. Actually, I talked the club into hiring you. Saw you in New York last summer and...well, I thought you really swung!" She was talking nervously, fast, clipping her words, suddenly avoiding his eyes as if afraid to meet his gaze.

Glen found it impossible not to stare at her bustline, which now more than invited a man's gaze.

She was beautifully developed. Her figure was delightfully full, but her face was almost child-like. The combination was almost overwhelming.

During the last days and nights, Glen had thought a lot about Lynn Bennings. When alone in bed, he had found himself dreaming about Lynn, wondering what it might be like to make love to her; what it would feel like to hold her body close to his own, to kiss her throat, to caress her breasts, to experience the warmth of her flesh blending hotly with his own.

Oddly enough his thoughts were moved by a need for a romance that would involve more than mere sex. Why he wasn't quite sure.

Lynn Bennings was the daughter of a rich man. Considering that, it would be a perfect set-up for a guy in his profession who wanted to get ahead the easy way—with money behind him. Yet, he was not that kind of man. And more to the point, Lynn was to him the kind of girl who didn't seem to be just a casual one night stand. And, oddly enough, she turned him on in more than a sexual way. Even if it was a good idea to get sex out of the way to discover if there was more beyond that attraction.

Suddenly Glen found himself standing closer to her. How he had crossed the half dozen feet between them, he didn't know. All at once he was only inches from her.

Lynn looked up into his eyes like a little girl. For a moment her lips parted as if to say something, or awaiting a kiss, and then she closed her mouth and stepped back, turning away.

"I'd better show you where to set up your men. It's in the ballroom." Lynn was already moving across the room. Her stride was slow and strangely awkward, as if she were fighting an inner war with herself and wasn't quite sure she wanted to walk away from him. That one look in her eyes had been pleading again; pleading and asking him something. What?

She led the way toward another doorway that opened to a short hall that ended in another door.

"In here is where the party will really swing," she announced, stepping into a hugely proportioned room.

A large counter bar had been placed on one side of the room; opposite it was a baby grand piano and empty space with three chairs lined against the wall. Lynn pointed in that direction.

"That's where the combo will be. In front people can dance or just gather in groups," she explained.

"How long is the thing going to last?" Glen inquired.

"Probably late—around twelve or later. It starts at three, which is just a little while yet. I have to run up and change, but that won't take long, since I have everything organized. I've just been waiting until you arrived. I wanted to see you and—"

Lynn broke off, her face flushed red.

Then after a moment she said: "Well, in any case, I did want to see you. I hope that...well, we'll have some time during the evening to get a chance to talk. I'm crazy about jazz, and I guess you have a lot of stories to tell..."

Again her voice broke and she looked away. "I keep getting my mouth all stuffed up with my foot!" she laughed nervously, turning to face him.

Glen found it impossible to keep from stepping closer. His hands were just about to reach out and pull her into his arms, when a tall older woman stepped into the room.

Glen stepped back, suddenly embarrassed.

What the hell had made him do that? he wondered. Then he saw the look in Lynn's eyes and knew. She had wanted him to kiss her. She had been waiting for such a move on his part. Why? For kicks? The young rich girl wanting to ball it with a jazz musician to see how different it was? It couldn't be much more. Or could it?

Again the doubts spun in. Was she just a rich girl looking for kicks or some innocent with a crush on the "fab musician"? Or simply a jazz fan?

He didn't know; couldn't, yet. But he was determined to find out.

The older woman stepped across the room toward them. There was a half hidden expression in her eyes that told him she'd guessed what almost happened.

"You'd better go up and get dressed, dear," the woman said in a cultured, controlled voice. She turned her attention toward Glen. "I'm Mercedes Bennings."

Glen looked at the woman, carefully trying to judge her as a mother and as a female. It was impossible. She was attractive; well kept for her age. A silver-gray streak cut across her hair in a most attractive way. She had high, yet well-formed breasts. It was hard to tell her exact age.

For a moment Lynn stared at Glen and then turned and left the room.

There was a short silence and then Mrs. Bennings said: "I see my daughter is quite taken by you."

"Oh?"

"You hadn't noticed?" An eyebrow arched. "Of course not. I'm sure."

"I've notice." He shrugged, then reconsidered, saying: "What business is that of yours? She's a lovely person, I'm sure. But certainly not a child. And has a mind of her own. Don't you think?"

"I think you're a sophisticated man. And you've been around the block, so to speak. I'm a mother. Get my point?"

"Not really…"

"Oh, come now, Mr. Fletcher. Between the two of us, you surely noticed. Lynn is a young girl. Somewhat taken by…what you represent, I suppose. But if I were you, I wouldn't get too close—too involved. Somebody might get hurt, and…"

Angrily he broke in with: "Is that a threat?"

"No. Hardly from me, anyway."

"Then I don't understand."

She sighed, then looking directly into his eyes, said: "Let's cut the crap! Okay? I'll be frank. It might be better if you simply kept your hands where they belonged…so to speak…on your trumpet. Not taking advantage of…well and impressionable young woman with a childish…whatever you call it nowadays."

"I wouldn't have the least idea," he countered, neither angrily nor amused. In fact he was a bit puzzled by the woman.

"Oh, come on, now!" She sounded quite honestly frustrated. "She thinks a lot of you…let's leave it at that. She might be flirtatious, but don't play into it. Please. As a favor."

"To you?"

"Of course."

"And what's in it for me?" he tossed back, wondering just what kind of game the woman was playing. That question crossed a socially polite line, but he didn't really give a damn.

"Oh, come on! Don't be silly!" She looked nervous, uncertain. "That's not the point!"

"Then what is?"

Without hesitation she retorted: "Well, let's say her father is very protective toward her. I'm a woman. I understand certain things that Earl can't."

"Oh? What things...do you understand?" He was now almost amused.

"Things. You're world is different from the one she grew up in. I know you musicians have different standards and—"

"Oh? Really! I should be insulted, I supposed." He suddenly felt amused by the exchange.

She continued, very seriously: "This is a small town and the people here are pretty much supportive and protective of my husband's...well...interests. He is a very...tough nut if crossed. Be warned, is my best advice."

"Again that sounds like a threat!" But this time he was less alarmed—and not in any way feeling threatened by her words.

"Well...frankly...never mind that. Enough that you know...well..."

She hesitated, nervously staring up at him; then continued. "Ever since your group came into town, Lynn has talked about nothing else. I hope you're wise enough *not* to take advantage of her...*and you know what I mean!* There are other women to… make such moves on. To be blunt about it."

There was a strange expression in the woman's eyes. They softened and she smiled, almost warmly.

"Would you have a cigarette?"

The sudden change of subject startled Glen. For a moment he stood there, speechless. Then he finally said: "Sure."

As he was lighting her cigarette, Mercedes Bennings leaned closer to him; her eyes looked up into his, almost intimately.

"How old would you say I am?" she suddenly asked.

That startled him. Suddenly she had changed from mother to what? Vamp? Flirtatious? He let his eyes sweep over her figure. She was a very attractive woman. Slim and sharp. He finally replied with: "You're a very attractive woman. It's hard to say."

"Well, I'm young enough and...aware that men find me attractive." The implication was all too blunt.

"I would imagine," Glen offered carefully.

For a moment the woman stood there staring at him. Then she blew smoke in his face. It was done in such a way as to seem possibly accidental. Glen guessed it to be on purpose.

"Mr. Fletcher, I was trying to make a point!" she announced.

"I think you made your point," Glen snapped almost angrily.

"I don't think I did!" she countered, moving closer. "When I want something—I get it. In that way I'm like my husband!"

"What is it you want?" Glen inquired carefully.

"I'm not quite sure—exactly. But it is my birthday, and I might ask for a special number from the great Glen Fletcher!" She smiled crookedly. "Is there anything really so wrong with that?"

"Look, Mrs. Bennings, I don't know what you have in mind, but let's understand each other." Glen took a deep breath and then said: "There are certain things that can be taken lightly, others must be accepted as quite serious. If I were you, I'd consider that before you request...the wrong number!"

Mercedes Bennings opened her mouth and laughed in his face.

"I like you, Glen Fletcher! I like you a lot!"

And with that the woman whipped around and glided across the room. A moment later he was alone.

MIDNIGHT LOVERS, BY CHARLES NUETZEL

Chapter Five

Even though Mercedes Bennings was going about doing her social duty playing the hostess, her thoughts kept centering more around Glen Fletcher.

The man impressed her. And there were so many reasons for finding out what kind of guy he was. The motives were important.

Lynn was, basically, inexperienced about men. Maybe her daughter might not be a virgin, but that didn't mean she could really know how a man could take advantage of a young woman.

Mercedes knew. And it had been a bitter experience.

Most men in Glen's profession took girls as they took cigarettes. They smoked them and then put the butt out in an ashtray, not caring what happened after that.

If he'd been only interested in cheap thrills then there was no reason why he wouldn't have picked up on her suggestive offer—no matter how subtle it might have been made.

The fact was he hadn't really indicated his reaction towards Lynn. If he played her, that was something Lynn was old enough to handle. She had to learn the facts of the real world one way or another.

Nothing to stop that.

Though her father was not as liberal, nor as generous. He was something else.

Mercedes shuddered at the thought of her husband's ability to strike out violently at anything that might threaten his family—especially his daughter.

It was a danger she'd tried to suggest to Glen Fletcher. Maybe she should have been more blunt. The man had impressed her. She was sure he wouldn't let threats stop him from going after what he really wanted. If he wanted Lynn, there was little anybody could do to stop it. One way or the other it was impossible to protect her daughter from the world. Nor men on the make. Lynn wasn't stupid; just young.

Mercedes sighed, mentally hoping everything would work out for the best. Perhaps nothing would happen at all. If things got complicated, maybe it would be possible for her to intervene. If not: God help everybody concerned!

* * * * * * *

The house had filled up fast after three o'clock. The musicians had arrived a little before the hour and they'd set up for playing. By six in the evening the room was crowded with guests; some were dancing, others merely sopped up the free booze and chattered drunkenly in little tight groups. His combo had taken several breaks and he was about to take another when Lynn Bennings came up to him and said: "Could I see you?" He nodded, blew a quick bridge and cut into the ending of *Laura.* As he moved the trumpet from his lips, he turned to the musicians.

"Take five."

Lynn asked: "Can't you make it longer?"

Glen turned, questioned her with his eyes.

"An hour or so?" she suggested. His amazement must have revealed itself. "It's about time you fellows had a little fun, too. The whole town's here—well, almost the whole town—and why shouldn't you get a break?" she offered, smiling.

Lynn had on a red cocktail dress that dipped revealingly low at the front to expose the white swells of her breasts in a most inviting and intriguing way. It was the best view he'd gotten of her neckline.

"I'm not one to argue with the boss!" Glen grinned. He turned to the boys. "Take a long break. I'll blow a few notes on the horn when I want you guys."

Lynn took his arm and said: "Make yourself at home. Eat and drink all you want."

"Hey, wait a minute. My boys will take that literally."

"So?"

"So they won't blow anything good after that!" Glen pointed out.

"I don't think anybody would notice by then, anyway." Lynn tugged him away from the bandstand.

"Where you taking me?" he inquired, pleased by her nearness. The soft feel of her fingers against his arm was most exciting.

They made their way through the crowds of people to the bar.

"What'll you have? A Scotch?" she inquired, squeezing his arm.

Glen looked at the woman and felt a deep sense of excitement generate through him.

"Anything," he finally said.

Lynn picked up a bottle of Scotch and then told him to take two glasses.

"Outside," she instructed.

Glen followed, his thoughts generating from warm to white hot. The nearness of Lynn, the excitement she created within him, was overpowering.

They walked through au open doorway and onto a patio. There was a scattering of people outside, some gathered around tables, others just gathered around each other.

Lynn led the way across the patio and onto the large lawn to the poolside. She chose a table that was some distance from the rest, as far from the house as possible.

They sat and she took the glasses, poured generous portions of Scotch into each and then handed him one.

This time he was ready for her when she tapped the glass.

"Well, here's to you!" she murmured softly, taking a sip of Scotch.

After a moment's silence Glen asked: "Well now, what next?"

She smiled, amused, and for the first time she looked like a fully mature woman who was in complete control of a situation. Women had a talent for pulling that trick with men. They always had the edge because it was the woman who made the advances, who did the seduction. The more skillful women managed to make the man believe he was the chaser, but nothing could be further from the

44

truth.

"I just wanted to talk. To get to know you better," she finally said in her low voice.

Glen studied her. The night had just fallen over the world, and stars were just starting to flicker into place. The moon was cut in half, casting only dim highlights on the right side of Lynn's face. The house lights painted a soft glow on her features, creating an artistic and beautiful picture.

How lovely she looks, Glen thought. *A goddess of beauty.*

It had been a long, long time since a woman had affected him in such a way. He felt more than mere physical attraction towards her. It was as if in her presence a magic settled over him, soothing, caressing, teasing.

As he sat there, Glen remembered Mercedes Bennings' words to him; remembered the implications about Lynn and her feelings toward him. It was impossible not to be affected by them; knowing that this woman no doubt was quite taken by him.

Under these circumstance it was his habit to take advantage of the situation.

"I've followed you quite a bit," Lynn finally said, running her fingers along the rim of her glass.

"That's nice to hear. The group needs fans." Glen took out a pack of cigarettes and then offered her one. As he lighted up for both of them Lynn looked boldly into his eyes.

"I hope you don't think I'm some spoiled young rich girl," she said after taking a deep drag on her cigarette.

"Why should I?"

"Well, most guys either think that, or are after

my money."

"1 didn't know you had money," Glen grinned, looking along her body in a most pointedly mocking way.

She shivered. "You shouldn't do things like that!"

"Like what?" he asked innocently.

"Look at me like that. I'm a nice girl," she laughed. "Very nice!"

"Of course you are. One of the nicest girls I've ever seen. One of the most beautiful ones, too." He took a sip of his drink.

"I bet you say that to all the girls!" she coyly pouted. But her eyes were twinkling like merry stars.

"Not to all of them," he assured her. "Only the beautiful ones."

"And how many of them are there?" she inquired teasingly.

"Oh, let me see...maybe a hundred thousand million—give or take ten or twenty."

They both laughed and then after a moment sat there staring silently at one another.

The mood changed so slowly, so subtly, that he didn't know when it had become quite serious and sensual. They were staring at each other in that searching silent way for a long time, and suddenly he found himself caught by a deep, all-embracing emotion that had little to do with mere sex. Yet he wanted to pull her into his arms, hold her close, comforting, protectively.

Now that was a very strange reaction! Normally all he considered was getting a woman's dress off and ravishing her body with passionate kisses.

46

Instead he merely sat there, fascinated by her.

Lynn was first to break the silence. "I think you're fun, Glen."

He liked the way she said his name, as if caressing it.

"You're fun, too."

Silence. Awkward silence. What they were saying made no sense at all. It was chatter to fill in the silence. What was really going on was something far subtler. Nothing really needed to be said to communicate the emotional feelings that were building up inside him—and perhaps in her.

She put out her cigarette and then finished off the drink. "Want another?"

Glen took his glass and emptied it. The liquor burned through his throat and settled at the pit of his stomach. He nodded and she refilled his glass.

"You folks are sure free with the booze," he observed, reaching out and impulsively touching her hand.

The contact made conversation useless. The contact suddenly was communication so complete that they sat there for sometime, feeling the sensations rushing over them like fiery waves.

Then suddenly they both stood as one. It all happened so fast. No time to think. Somehow they were united in a way that was totally alien to anything in his past experience. Suddenly they slipped into each other's arms. Glen wasn't even aware of what was happening until her lips reached up under his and made contact.

It was one of those sweet, innocent kisses that cut deep. A light touching of lips, a light, gentle pressing of bodies that said all there was to say, gave all there was to give. A melting of bodies and souls; a meeting of mind, emotion and desire. Gentle magic that was complete in itself.

The soft feel of her yielding lips under his was like the taste of a sweet wine; delicious heady wine that reached throughout his whole being.

Gently they slipped away from the embrace and Lynn stood there as if hypnotized, gazing up into his eyes with all the sweet beauty of love on her face.

"I didn't mean..." Glen started to say, then broke off knowing that it was exactly what he had meant to do.

Without a word Lynn took hold of his hand and pulled him around the pool, back toward the expansive garden. They moved down a narrow pathway between rose bushes and then turned to the right. Suddenly they were in a world away from everybody else, a new, beautiful world of soft colors and scented perfumed air. She came into his arms yieldingly; her lips opened under his as her body slowly tensed.

The kiss had fire and softness, violence and tenderness all mixed together so beautifully that he was left dazed. Her tongue reached deep into his mouth and then withdrew. He tasted of her lips, her teeth, then into the depths of her mouth. Never had he experienced anything so wonderful, so gentle and savage and passionate at the same time. His head was throbbing, the blood rushed through him like liquid fire, and his breathing hammered in his lungs.

"Oh, Glen," Lynn murmured as they pressed their cheeks together. "I didn't know it would happen like this...so fast!"

He had a million questions to ask her; a million

48

answers to get. But all he could think of was the softness held so close to him, the child-like, full womanly body that hugged to his.

Finally, Lynn stepped a few inches back. For a moment neither of them said anything.

"Glen, I won't say I didn't want that to happen," she finally told him in a low breathless voice. "I did with all my heart."

Strangely he wasn't telling her all the things he had told so many other women who had so obviously gotten a crush on him. He didn't tell her that it would be a mistake to expect anything other than a quick fiery romance. He couldn't say that, because suddenly he didn't believe it.

What was happening would happen, and would continue to happen.

After a moment. Glen shook himself, as if trying to get out of a daze.

"Look," he finally said, "I don't know what you have in mind but—"

"Nothing," Lynn quickly said. "What could I have in mind?"

"I don't know..."

"Glen?"

"Yes."

"I..." She hesitated and then continued awkwardly. "I...want you to know...that I'm not...I don't throw myself at men. I don't know what's happening. I don't understand it."

"Don't try to." He stood there attempting to find the words, attempting to decide what should be said. Instead, Glen reached for her, pulled her close, and caressed her hair, kissed her forehead.

Yes, he thought with deep emotion, *something*

was happening. Much too fast. Impossibly!

Fantastically!

After a quick kiss Lynn pushed away, turned.

"I don't...think we should stay out here. I mean..." She started to push past him, but Glen grabbed hold of her.

"Wait!"

"Please," she pleaded.

"What's wrong?"

"Everything is wrong!" she told him in a shaky voice. "This is all wrong. I shouldn't have let it happen. I'm sorry."

"Why?"

"Because. Dad wouldn't let anything...well, he'd be against anything like...this."

"Like what, Lynn?" Glen demanded, determined to make her come right out and say exactly what she meant. Suddenly it was very important to him.

"Like *us*!" Lynn announced, looking up into his eyes like a lost child.

"You're over twenty-one..."

"Yes, but—"

"But nothing! Hell, Lynn. You're a woman. Don't tell me you let your father run your life?"

"I—"

"What kind of hold could he have on you?"

"You just don't understand," Lynn told him in an emotionally choked voice. Her head hung, her eyes lowered to her feet.

"Understand what?"

"About a girl in my position. There are...well, he has a lot of money, and wants...well, this is all so silly. What are we talking about anyway?" she inquired. "After all, what's a kiss?"

50

"I think you know," Glen offered. "With some people it's nothing. With others it can mean a lot."

"Meaning?" It was her turn to push him into commitments.

"Lynn, it...it means just that. Something happened—fast. I don't quite understand it myself. But...what happened was important. I want to see you again. I want to know you better." He pulled her close, but she was stiff in his arms.

"I don't know," she murmured. "It's all been really so silly. Right from the start. I see you on the bandstand and...maybe people are...can they be attracted to one another that fast?"

"Don't ask me." Silence, then: "We can see each other?"

"Why?"

"Because I want to see you again."

"My money?" she inquired in a breathless voice, as if afraid that might be it.

"For your money. Just your money. What else would a man like me want to see an attractive woman for? You ask too many questions!"

She looked surprised, almost startled. They stared at one another for a long moment, then something seemed to click, connect, as if a switch had been yanked into place and their minds were locked in a very intimate embrace, surrounding one another, merging.

Suddenly they both knew something very special about one another, and about what had happened. They both silently recognized the truth. Whatever that might be; an illusive and yet very powerful magnetic need for closeness had united them—for connection. They both knew it had to be continued—and would never be satisfied by mere conversation, yet had to begin there.

Like two kids, they hugged, then parted.

They both laughed and without a word returned to the table. A little later they went into the house.

Chapter Six

Glen picked up a few small cocktail sandwiches and then returned to the "bandstand," swallowed down the last sandwich and then reached for his trumpet.

The evening had dragged on, and he was glad when the last set was over. Glen went through the house, looking for Lynn, but didn't find her. When he inquired, the butler said that Miss Bennings had gone to bed.

Glen shrugged, and then got his trumpet.

Some ten minutes later he walked into his hotel room, closed the door and was undressing when there was a soft knocking on the door.

The first thought that ran through his mind was that it would be Lynn. Ever since she had left him earlier that evening his thoughts had been on nothing else. They had made general plans on getting together some time but no specific date had been arranged. Glen had been so sure of seeing her again this evening that it never entered his mind that he should have made a definite date.

As he opened the door, Ivy Turner walked in.

She had on a bathrobe that hugged around her sexy figure like a skin-tight glove. He didn't need any more than one quick glance to see there wasn't anything on underneath the robe.

"How'd it go?" Ivy inquired, sitting down on the bed.

Glen knew what Ivy would want: a little private party. She'd been left alone all day; and if that wasn't bad enough, they'd missed playing games the night before because he was too tired for anything but hitting the sack.

"Fine. A long party, but..." Glen shrugged, letting his eyes flow over Ivy's body. She was sexy as hell, but nothing more.

"I had a dragging day, Glen," she told him bitterly, opening the front of her robe. "I missed you."

"I bet you did!" Glen laughed, suddenly perversely glad she was there. He hadn't actually looked forward to spending the long night alone, thinking about Lynn, dreaming about making love to her. And he was half loaded, to boot.

Now, with the raging desire for Lynn already hot in his blood, exhausted as he felt, Glen was glad to have company. Ivy would focus his mind.

The woman sat there, waiting, her robe parted at the top, exposing the rounded curve of one breast, with its pink point large and inviting.

She would be good for him right then; yet he hesitated.

Ivy stood and let the robe fall completely open. Her breasts pushed out, naked to his gaze.

"You're a strange woman, Ivy," Glen said, stepping over to the desk and opening the bottle of whiskey sitting there.

"Why do you say that?" she inquired, coming up beside him, pressing her breast into his arm. The

54

soft feel of that large cushion of flesh sparked an automatic need.

"Well, here are you...after a long day alone...you give yourself freely, and for what? Just kicks. And—"

Ivy slipped her hands around his body, pressed up against his back.

"Who ever gave you that idea?" she demanded.

Glen didn't say anything. He was only aware of the softness of the woman's breasts against his back.

"I've been crazy about you ever since we first met," Ivy announced, pressing against him.

"Crazy mad about you!" she murmured, kissing the back of his neck.

Glen turned, pulling her into his arms and covering her lips. Ivy's tongue darted out, fiery; her body tensed. Their tongues moved together in a savage dance.

He felt the woman squirm against him greedily. Her thigh pressed demandingly between his legs.

Then he remembered Lynn Bennings. He froze momentarily; then his tongue was drawn deep into Ivy's mouth and he tensed against the hotness of the kiss.

After a long time, Ivy stepped out of the embrace, slipped out of her robe and stood before him, completely naked.

His eyes wandered over her body, fascinated as he had always been.

Her breasts were large, well-supported, lovely. Her red hair silky. Her features invited him to make love to every inch of her.

What else did a man need?

"Oh, Glen, if you only knew..." she sighed, her

breasts heaving.

"What?" he managed in a low rasp.

"Nothing..." Her voice was small, distant. Shrugging, Ivy bounced to the bed and plopped down, lying on her back in silent offering.

Glen reached for the bottle of whiskey again and then poured himself a strong. stiff drink.

As he sipped the whiskey Glen felt a vague sense of guilt at what was now about to take place. He couldn't help wondering what Lynn' would think if she knew that he was about to make love to another woman.

Any woman to share his bed.

It didn't matter that Ivy had been doing just that even since they'd met.

Somehow he felt connected in a special way with Lynn.

And that, surely, was illusion. They didn't even know one another.

Yet, how he wanted her.

Angrily he shoved that thought away.

It was foolish to think about Lynn in such a way. They had kissed and now he was acting like a stupid innocent school kid with a teenage crush. There was nothing between them but a kiss and a little conversation.

He'd been making love to Ivy for months now. There were, between the two of them, so many things—too many to count. They were in the same business; they enjoyed unrestricted intimacy. Why should he feel guilty about making love to Ivy? It should be the other way around! He should feel guilty for having kissed Lynn.

Glen gulped the whiskey and then turned and

faced Ivy.

For a moment Glen looked at Ivy, let his eyes run over the peaks of her breasts, across her flat stomach, over her wide hips, along her tapered, full thighs and legs.

"What's taking you so long, love?" Ivy inquired, looking puzzled. "I'm hungry…for you know what! What's keeping you?"

"Nothing!" Glen slammed the glass on the desk and then started undressing. His eyes never left Ivy. He tried to keep his thoughts as focused her vision.

A few moments later Glen slipped down on the bed and folded the woman in his arms.

They kissed, gently, carefully. They hugged together like two romantic lovers, aware of the physical contact, the warmth of flesh.

He moved. His lips caressed her flesh, felt it tenderly with the point of his tongue. Ivy tensed against the kiss. A wildness surged through him. He felt her squirm, grip him tighter. His hands moved over her excitedly.

"Oh, Glen..." she moaned. "Glen!"

Her hands reached greedily for him.

When he found lips she sobbed in pleasure.

Then the image of another woman flashed across his mind. Lynn Bennings. Mentally he saw her beautiful face, examined every detail; the up-swept nose, the silken-black hair, the lovely body. And he remembered the kiss that had been so sweet, and been more than all he had ever experienced before in his life with any woman.

And suddenly he felt cheap and ashamed at being with Ivy.

The woman moved, sensually against him. Glen

wanted to stop her, wanted to tell Ivy to go away and leave him alone.

All at once she gasped and clamped her legs tight about him, and he felt himself being literally enveloped into her warm embrace. It didn't take long after that. Ivy wouldn't let him move slowly. In that moment he realized the harsh truth: Women like Ivy fit into his life-style, but not Lynn Bennings. Ivy Turner was just right for him. They were good for each other. He was a fool for even having thought seriously about Lynn; a total stranger. His life was music. And Ivy with her hot, hungry body, free-wheeling sex was all he should need or want.

He focused on her lush, soft, hot flesh, the squirming, demanding hunger embracing him so frantically. She was literally moaning in the pleasure of their nearness.

Then he heard her scream in an anguished voice, tense with pleasure.

"Oh love, I love you. Oh, God...Glen...Glen... Glen...Oh, Glen!"

The words were uttered between rapid thrusts of her hips.

He let himself ride on the naked raw animal sensations, without thinking about anything. It was a ride from reality. Nothing more And suddenly he didn't care about Lynn Bennings; all he knew was the building sensation of total pleasure in Ivy's wildly churning body. In the last moments they both strained furiously together, locking in an almost violent final embrace.

Then her body fell away alongside his. Her lips covered his face with love-kisses, as she spoke between them.

"Glen, Glen I love you...love you!"

MIDNIGHT LOVERS, BY CHARLES NUETZEL

Chapter Seven

Glen was between breaks, taking a smoke outside in the back of the club when a small, low voice called his name.

"Glen Fletcher?"

He turned, startled.

Lynn Bennings stood there in a blue cocktail dress. Her hair was done up on her head, giving a regal, sophisticated look. The thrust of her breasts was only suggested in the fluffy design of the dress.

"Well, where have you been?" he inquired, pleased to see her: much more pleased than he liked to think. The last couple of days had been an anguished torment. He had wanted to call Lynn, but something had always held him off and then the evenings had been with Ivy.

Lynn was silent for a long time and the moonlight played with her features, painting them with soft lights, caressing over the lines of her face like some artist had created a masterpiece.

God, she looks beautiful, he thought, trying to hold back the emotion that flooded over him.

"I didn't want to come, Glen," she finally said, stepping forward. She stopped a few inches away from him.

"Why?"

She laughed. "Why do you think?"

Silence. Then she said, "I couldn't keep away. The other day—Sunday—after you went back to work I...well, I chickened out and made myself scarce. I'm a silly fool."

"No. No, you aren't," Glen told her, reaching and pulling her against him. "You're wonderful."

He tried to kiss her but Lynn stepped back, out of his arms. "Okay, let's start from the beginning. I'll start out honest. I was attracted to you. I arranged to have you hired—and then I got frightened. That's over now."

She was silent for a moment and then added: "You were right about me. And I shouldn't be afraid of Dad. Well, what I mean..."

Her voice faded out, and she looked away as if embarrassed.

Glen stood there, thinking. He tried to tell himself this was all crazy; that Lynn was all wrong for him. But he didn't believe it.

"Well, where now?" he asked.

"I thought we might get together this evening. After all, you asked me out. Now I'm accepting." She smiled happily, like a little child who has just received a piece of candy for a cute little trick.

"After the show, a night lunch?" he offered, feeling an excited tingle rush over him.

"Fine. Wonderful!" Lynn cried, throwing her arms around his neck and pressing close.

Just then Ivy stepped outside.

"Well, what's this?" she inquired in a cold, flat voice.

They broke away from each other.

62

There was a long awkward silence and then Glen said: "This is Lynn Bennings, Ivy. Ivy Turner, our singer."

"Yes, I've seen her," Lynn announced in a hostile voice. "You're really great!"

"Thanks," was all Ivy said.

The two women stared at one another for a short moment. It seemed to Glen that sparks were silently flashing between the two.

Ivy finally said: "Well, I didn't mean to break anything up, but we have to go on!"

"I'd better leave," Lynn offered. "I'll have a table out front. I'll be watching every moment of your music."

With that she left.

Ivy stared after her like a jungle cat about to spring on its enemy.

"What's that?" Ivy snapped, turning to Glen.

Glen shrugged, tried to avoid Ivy's eyes.

"Look...I don't think like it, Glen," Ivy announced coldly. "If she's just some chick on the make—"

"Shut up!" Glen snapped.

"Don't say that to me, Glen!" she told him in a soft voice.

They stared at one another for a moment and then Ivy smiled. It was a forced action of her lips. "I should worry, love."

She grabbed hold of Glen's arm and led him to the back door that led behind the bandstand.

* * * * * * *

Lynn Bennings watched the combo playing

63

through the arrangements, feeling a thrill at knowing she would be with Glen Fletcher a little later.

Ever since she had seen him that first time months before, Lynn had been fascinated. There was something about the man, both his carriage and his looks, that completely possessed her. So many nights she had dreamed about him, thought about being held in his arms. Maybe it was simply a school girl crush kind of thing, or fan taken by a celebrity. But it had grown. It was as if something special had clicked, as if the two of them were lost souls who had found one another. She had never believed in love at first sight, but the way things were developing between them it almost seemed as if that might be possible. At least as far as she was concerned. Was there such a thing as soul mates? A part of her wanted to believe that. And if that was so: was this man her long lost lover from a past life? Maybe many past lives? She hardly believed in such supernatural stuff; but somehow something very special was happening. Maybe it was the same with all love relationships; a person believed what was happening to them was magic and different and world shattering.

Lynn was old enough to know the signs. She'd been in love only once before, and that was when she was eighteen. That seemed like ages ago. And it was different. But it was her first affair. There had been other men in her life, some of whom had been paid by her father to leave and never come back. And they were different, too.

As she thought about past affairs, Lynn felt the bitter hatred cut deep through her. To Earl Bennings there wasn't a man alive good enough for his daughter. She had lived in continued terror of her father for years, and it wasn't until the other night when Glen Fletcher had talked to her about it that she'd realized how much terror had controlled every action she'd taken. Every man she had fallen for had become a secret, hidden romance. Even from the first young kid who had seduced her on a date when she was in high school.

All she could really remember about that night was being dazed in a sea of sensation, one more thrilling than the last. Her weak attempts to stop him became less and less meaningful, until she was sobbing for him to continue. All the time her mind was mentally screaming this was all wrong. She didn't have any protection. She might get pregnant. What would her parents think? How would she feel about it the next morning?

Later that night she had cried a long time, almost silently, in bed. She never told her folks about what had happened.

Lynn didn't fool herself about herself. The life Lynn's family had been able to afford had come close to spoiling her when she was a teenager, but in college, being exposed to other people from all walks of life, she had come down several pegs. Then she had met John Clark and fell in love for the first time. Every other guy before that had been merely a try-out, affair. He came from a poor family and had worked his way through college. Maybe that was part of her reason for becoming so emotionally attached. She had discovered a man who was smart, a hard worker and anxious to get ahead. She'd been given all the advantages in life from her father. This young college man had to work for everything he had, which was damned little. Most of all he was a good lover—though it wouldn't have been important. It was with John that she learned the difference between sexual orgasm and sexual love where the love became more important. She wanted to help him. And because he needed help she felt for the first time in her life important, for her own sake, and needed. She felt for the first time in her life important, for her own sake, and needed.

Because she had money sent by her father it was possible to have an apartment. John lived with her on weekends and most of the nights. They were almost like man and wife.

Each time they made love it was the same thing. Only better. More fulfilling in a deep emotional and sensual way.

Then the shock came!

It was a terrible lesson in life that still had its effects on Lynn.

Up until then she had thought love meant something and would mean more than money, status.

She would have given up anything for John Clark.

The bitter lesson she learned drove her into the arms of many casual lovers, in a desperate attempt to forget the horrid bitterness of what happened because of her father. And for a woman even half as attractive as herself it wasn't at all difficult to find men willing to spend a long night of carnal orgasm with her. Only after a long time was she able to forget and become respectably selective in her love affairs.

When Earl Bennings discovered the romance, he had offered the boy ten thousand dollars—and that had been the end of that.

The event had hurt Lynn and left a mark on her that only time had numbed away.

When she returned home it had been necessary to keep all her affairs completely secret.

But now for the first time in her life, she wanted to be open and honest about her feelings and desires. She realized that this decision had come automatically. Why, she wasn't sure. But, regardless, if it was necessary she would force herself to fight for what she wanted, no matter what the cost.

Maybe it was Glen; maybe the age she had reached.

Maybe there was something to that silly old idea of soul mates meeting, falling in love and being together for the rest of their lives—and again and again over the centuries. A nice fantasy. A lovely idea.

But this was reality. And that, regardless, made a difference.

As long as she could remember, Lynn had dreamed of falling in love with a man like Glen Fletcher. She felt sure about Glen Fletcher. Why, she didn't quite understand. Hopefully it wasn't just wishing to make it so.

She had given a lot of thought to the matter; tried to convince herself it was merely the glamour of what he was. Sure, that helped, she admitted to herself. But, after all, she was a rich young woman, and show business didn't have to be anything so fantastic and unapproachable as it might be for some girl from a middle-class family.

Now, at twenty-five, she had passed her childhood, but it had taken Glen's statement about her being afraid of her father to snap her completely out of it.

You had to grab hold of life, fight for what you wanted, and not give up until it was hopeless. A child played games, flitting from one thing to another, afraid of getting hurt, afraid of losing.

Those thoughts about herself and her life had been strong and overwhelming during the last few days. When she'd learned that Glen Fletcher had finally arrived in town a week before, Lynn had made up her mind to do what ever was necessary to meet him. Then she'd almost been frightened off. Now she would fight for the man she wanted. What happened in the future she had no way of knowing. But what was fantastic to her was the fact that Glen seemed honestly interested. And because of that she could almost believe all these feelings were not illusion. Maybe, this time, they were real—and worth fighting for. If she was wrong, well at least she'd know she had fought for the truth.

And there were ways to get a man interested—even a man like Glen Fletcher. She realized this was for keeps.

Lynn watched him on the stage; watched Ivy Turner.

Jealousy knifed through her every time she looked at Ivy. She could only guess what was going on between the two of them, but she was quite certain they were past the holding hands stage.

The biggest mistake she could make was to give herself to Glen right off. But on the other hand, he wasn't the kind to just hold hands, either. He wanted a woman who would give of herself, both body and soul. But there were too many who were quite anxious to bed down with men like him. Lynn realized that. What she did would have to be handled with care, carefully planned out.

Lynn had made up her mind completely about Glen Fletcher and herself.

A thrill waved through her at the thought.

Mrs. Glen Fletcher. Lynn Fletcher. It had a nice, beautiful sound to it.

The only thing she was afraid of was that her father's money would get in the way. But she put that thought out of her mind and centered her thoughts on the image of being the wife of a famous trumpet player. She could be a lot of help to him as a wife, even if she wouldn't help him in the least bit with any money she might get from her family. That was the worst thing that could happen.

It was a beautiful dream, Lynn realized, but a dream she'd had for a long time now.

What was love, anyway? A feeling between two people! Nobody knew another person until after living with them a long, long time. Everything in life was a gamble.

Glen Fletcher stepped up to her table and sat down. "Well, how are you doing?" he asked.

"Fine. Finished?" she asked.

"No. Another set and that'll do it." He was silent and then said, "Want another drink?"

She looked at her almost empty glass and nodded.

Glen motioned to the waiter, who came over to the table.

"Another for Miss Bennings. Give me a beer."

He reached out and folded his hand over hers. "I should think it would be a drag waiting here this long."

"Oh, no! You don't know how exciting it is. I used to come here every, week, just sit and listen to the music. I'm quite a jazz lover."

"We don't really play jazz here. Sorta a jazzy dance music. You'll have to come when we do a session for kicks." His lips were speaking, but the expression in his eyes seemed to be saying something completely different.

"It sounds like jazz to me," Lynn announced firmly, smiling.

"Well, a little. But you gotta keep it commercial for the customers. Nothing progressive, you know."

"Oh, well, if you mean that, I understand."

The drinks came and they started talking about jazz, dance bands, music in general. To Lynn it was fascinating.

"Things have changed in the last years," he said. "Ten years ago you could really have a swinging ball. There would be jam sessions every week and the musicians would get together at a spot like this—usually in Los Angeles or New York and a few other towns across the country—and really blow. Today the sessions are watered down for the public. Then you could learn something—it was a work shop for musicians. Now everything is written down, organized. Oh, there are a few things now and then that are exciting. But it's not the working school it used to be. I learned a lot from jamming. Worked with some big names at the time. But..." He shrugged, took a sip of his beer. "I guess that's not very interesting to you."

"Yes it really is. Tell me something more, anything. Anything at all."

70

He squeezed her hand and was about to say something when Ivy Turner came over and sat down.

"Cozy," she observed, lighting a cigarette.

Lynn looked into the woman's eyes and felt a coldness hidden there. Yet, she realized, no doubt this woman was quite nice, under normal circumstances, There wasn't anything hard or nasty in her eyes; merely the look of one female engaging another female over a man.

All was fair in love and war. And this was both.

Lynn said: "Glen, where you taking me afterwards?"

The remark was made for Ivy's sake.

"Oh, there's a place just outside of town—"

"Benny's Club?" Lynn asked.

"Yes. They have...hell, you probably know the place."

"Love it."

Ivy watched the conversation with narrowed eyes. There was a hurt, distant expression on her face. Finally she said, "Well, don't let me break up anything."

With that she left.

An awkward silence followed. Then Lynn asked: "Your girl friend?"

Glen hesitated and then said: "You can't be around a woman like Ivy without noticing her."

"I guess not," Lynn agreed.

"No strings, though—if that's what you mean," he quickly told her.

The expression in his eyes became suddenly confused, as if he realized what he'd just said was a little out of place, considering they hardly knew each other. It had revealed a lot to Lynn.

She smiled at him and patted his hand. "I'm glad."

A short silence, then Glen said: "I'd better get back."

With that Glen stood, said he'd see her later, and then returned to the stage.

Lynn watched, enthralled, until the long set was finished and the man stepped down from the stage and once more walked across the dance floor to her table, a wide, eager look in his eyes.

Chapter Eight

To Glen, the night lunch at the restaurant was so completely different from the ones he had shared with Ivy so many times in the past—and other girls like Ivy. They ate mostly in silence, merely communicating with their eyes. There was a little light conversation, but it was merely polite attempts to break the heavy silence. Glen merely dabbled with his ham and eggs and sipped half his cup of coffee. Cigarettes burned up like paper thrown on a roaring fire. The ashtray filled and was unloaded a couple of times by the alert waitress.

Every time Glen looked into Lynn's dark-brown eyes he felt a shiver of excitement and weakness rush through him and he would reach for another cigarette. He wasn't quite sure when they had finished with their meal. They merely sat there in the semi-darkness of the atmospheric all-night dinner club and enjoyed the quiet silence of their company with each other. It was strange and new; an experience he'd never known before. A silent communication of eyes that said so much.

Finally Glen reached across the table and folded Lynn's hand in his. A light trembling of her lips pulled up into a contented smile; her eyes seemed to brighten like little stars.

Glen said, "I don't know why I'm in such a quiet mood. Normally I try to keep conversation raging..."

Lynn laughed. "You're smoking a lot—maybe that's the reason."

He shook his head. "Nervous—under the surface; that's all."

"Glen," she began in a soft hesitant voice, "what happens now?"

The question startled Glen because he really hadn't given much thought about what would happen next. It was as if he were riding the night, letting some mystic god direct the action. With another woman it would have been quite simple; they would have left the restaurant and gone to either of their apartments—or hotel rooms—and spent the night together. Glen knew that was what he would desire with Lynn, yet it seemed strangely out of place to suggest such a thing to her; it would have seemed out of place to lower their feelings down to mere physical wanting.

"What did you expect to happen?" Glen offered softly.

She shrugged. "I didn't mean about tonight, if that's what you're getting at. I meant...between us?"

Glen backed away from that idea for a moment, looking at it from a mental distance.

What could happen between them? Where could they head? What would the ending be?

He was devoted to his music and to his career. Here was a rich young woman, possibly with only a crush on him. But assuming that it could be more,

74

would she be happy living with a musician who was traveling all over the country? Who worked nights and slept late into the morning and early afternoon? An upside down existence.

He said, "Lynn, do we have to think about that?"

"No," she answered, shaking her head slowly from side to side. "Maybe it was a foolish question."

Glen squeezed her hand tenderly and told her with his eyes that it was far from a foolish question.

After a little while Glen caught the attention of the waiter and when the man came to the table, paid the bill.

They got up, went outside and then slid into his car. He sat there behind the wheel, undecided, not knowing where he might go. Instinct, pure animal desire, said to go some place quiet where he might make violently passionate love to Lynn.

They drove for a long time before either of them said anything. It was Lynn, asking for a cigarette, that broke the silence. He pulled out a pack and handed it to her.

"Glen, you're afraid of me, aren't you?" Lynn finally said, after taking a deep puff of the cigarette.

"Why do you ask that?"

"The way you reacted to the kiss."

"What was wrong with it?"

"Nothing, really. But I can't help thinking you don't react like that to all the girls...like Ivy Turner, for example!" The last words were subtly biting, as if she were attempting to dig into his relationship with Ivy.

Glen was momentarily annoyed and then decided to get that subject out of the way right from the beginning.

"Ivy is around, Lynn...and I'd be a fool if I didn't let nature take its course. Ivy's attractive and—"

"I don't want to hear any more," she announced in an annoyed voice.

"You asked me and—"

"I don't want to hear about Ivy!" she snapped almost angrily. Then: "I'm sorry. I did ask for it. Only, no woman likes to...well...likes the idea of thinking about the man she's...with...sleeping with another woman!" She spat out the last part as if it were some dirty sentence that came hard to her lips.

The silence was awkward after that.

The road was dark, an endless strip of highway that stretched out before them into the night—into nothingness that kept creating itself before them and dissolving behind them.

It was as if they were in some timeless world where only they existed; where only a few phantom cars sped by like beacons waving in the darkness.

"Lynn, things between Ivy and me aren't serious. I want you to know that and understand that—"

"That you can sleep with woman and not think of it as being serious?" without emotion in her voice.

"That's not exactly true. You have to understand the way things are in this bloody business. I move from town to town, and there's a lot of loneliness. And a person will find love—in one form or another—any way they can. There's nothing wrong with that. We're not children playing at finding out what it's all about, and—"

"I don't need a lecture on what makes up an

adult!" she snapped back, putting out the cigarette and nervously lighting another. "We're off to a fine start!"

Glen continued driving until he came to a side road, up which he turned, drove a short distance and then stopped. He killed the engine and turned toward Lynn.

She smiled mockingly at him. "You must be kidding!"

For a moment he didn't quite understand the implication of her words. Then he felt embarrassment flush his face, and mentally gave thanks that it was dark so that she couldn't see the redness there.

"I wanted to talk to you, Lynn," he said seriously.

"What about—seduction?"

"No!"

She frowned and the dim glow of the moon made her face look beautiful as she looked at him. Her lips pouted, dimpling at the corners. Her eyes narrowed and then widened slightly.

Then, without a word she slipped closer to him, put out the cigarette and then slid her arms around his neck. "I don't want to argue with you, Glen."

"I'm not going to argue. I just want to make something very clear to you." He was suddenly very serious; he'd made up his mind about something, and that startled Glen.

"Lynn, I've never met a girl who struck me like you have, and—"

"I bet you say that to all your women," she murmured, brushing her lips along his cheek.

"No! Please, Lynn, try to listen...it's important!" Glen said, attempting to ignore her subtle advances.

"Is it really that important?" she said softly, caressing the lobe of his ear with her lips.

"Yes! I want you to understand something and—"

Her lips found his before he could say any more and the will crumbled under him. All he could do was melt against that kiss. His tongue dipped deep into the hollow of her mouth, tasting of the sweetness there, as he felt the soft pressure of her breasts cushioned against his chest.

How, oh how he wanted to make love to her right there, right now.

Gently he pushed her away and looked seriously into her eyes. "Lynn, you don't really know what you're doing!"

Lynn laughed.

"Are you kidding? I'm not some kid just out of school!" Her voice was low and even more husky than usual.

"I mean, Lynn, this is a fire-cracker we're sitting on, and if you keep pushing, it'll go off! I want you more than any woman I've ever known, but—"

"What?" she quickly asked.

"But...I don't know!"

He turned away, looked through the windshield, trying to fight back the rushing, building desire that was hammering at his temples, burning through his nerves and muscles.

What bothered Glen most of all was the fact that he knew it would be a simple matter to seduce Lynn right then and there. But he couldn't! Something kept screaming in his mind not to take advantage of the situation, not to cheapen the feeling he was experiencing, not to bring their relationship down to the mere animal passion.

He sat there arguing with himself, trying to understand exactly what it was he felt for this young woman. A sense of protectiveness, that much he admitted. A desire to come between her and any kind of hurt or harm. And maybe that was why he couldn't bring himself to cross the line too soon. He didn't really know how such a relationship would—could—end. Yet, Glen asked himself, why did he want to go out with her, continue to see her? All men wanted to seduce the woman they went out with—the prime motive of wanting a woman's company was a sexual desire for her. Sex came first; then emotional attachment followed. Get sex out of the way and you knew there was something more than mere physical desire between you and the woman.

He'd known a lot of women who, at first sight, seemed like something very special.

There had been a lot of strange bitches who crossed his life; women who wanted all kinds of different thrills. Each seemed, at times, in their own way, totally different from all the others.

Though, in the end, it was all the same. Orgasm for orgasm's sake. There came a time in every man's life when he had to decide which direction he wanted to take. And now, Glen realized he wanted something far more serious than orgasm.

Angrily Glen started the car, turned it around and headed back toward town.

Lynn sat next to Glen in stony silence. It wasn't until he turned down the road that led to her home that she spoke.

"You'd better go back to the club. That's where

I left the car," she said softly. Then after a moment "I thought there for a moment you were actually going to attempt to seduce me."

Glen's eyes looked to hers, trying to read what reaction she had to such an idea. Her features revealed nothing.

"Lynn—I won't say it didn't pass over my mind."

"Why didn't you, then?"

"I don't know. The only thing I know is that I feel different about you—different than I've felt about any other woman. But—I'll admit it—I'm afraid. But I don't know of what!"

Silence; then as he pulled the car in front of the club where his group was working, Lynn said:

"Glen, we're acting like a couple of school kids."

"I know!" He slammed on the brakes and killed the engine. "Okay, then, what is it you want?"

"You," she said simply. "And I want to play the game for keeps...or for whatever it can give us! But certainly not for a cheap tumble in bed."

Her eyes smiled tenderly at him. "Don't look so surprised. I don't throw myself around...and that shouldn't bother you in either case, since it is what we can be to one another that counts. Nothing more! I don't want to know about you and Ivy, and I don't want to know about any other women you might have made...taken to bed. All I want is every moment I can get with you!" Her arms slid around his neck and she pressed closer, looking into his eyes. "Glen, do I seem too bold, too brazen, too forward? I don't mean to. Only that one of us had to push the truth out into the open. Two people meet, and then they desire one another. We don't have the time—do we? You'll be leaving town in a couple of days. I know that, and I don't want—" She didn't complete the sentence because their lips met at that moment.

For a long time they embraced, for a long time they held their lips tightly together, their tongues dancing, their breaths heaving. Then slowly, as if coming up from under the water, they slipped away from each other.

"Take me to your room, Glen," Lynn said in a small voice.

Glen merely nodded, holding down the tight emotional choking sensation in his throat. Suddenly he was sure how he felt about Lynn; he was sure that once the sex was out of the way he would feel it even more strongly.

He started the car again and headed down the darkened street, coming to a stop in front of the Davis Hotel.

MIDNIGHT LOVERS, BY CHARLES NUETZEL

Chapter Nine

Ivy Turner watched as Glen talked to Lynn Bennings, and felt a terrible stab of anguish needle through her. She puffed deep on her cigarette and turned away, walking backstage.

She didn't like what was going on between Glen and that Bennings woman. Ivy had watched Glen play around with some of the town broads just for kicks. It was a side advantage of being young, healthy, good looking and in the public eye. A certain type of woman was willing to do anything to get the thrill of bedding down with a performer; and a lot of them were attractive enough to be impossible to ignore. Ivy herself had managed a couple of flings with male customers, but she usually kept to musicians and away from involvements with the public.

There had been one customer who had come on really weird. He had been sitting close to the bandstand and with a very attractive young woman. He invited her to join them at the next break. She ended up sitting between the woman and man. Drinks came. Conversation was led more by the young blonde who suddenly suggested: "Why don't you come over to our place for a drink after work?" Ivy had been used to blunt passes once in a while, but sounded wild. She didn't have a current boyfriend. She was sexually starved. Her memory of the couple's home was vague. They were anxious to have a threesome with her. By that time Ivy didn't give a damned hell about anything.

So she'd been around the barn, so to speak, and pretty much knew the score. She'd done her swinging. It wasn't the kind of love-life she wanted any more.

But ever since working for Glen Fletcher, Ivy had felt differently about herself and life. She had been charmed by his good looks, his sensitive love-making.

What bothered Ivy now was that Glen had been mentally detached from her ever since meeting Lynn Bennings. He had become preoccupied in his love-making, which wasn't like him.

Goddamn that Lynn Bennings! Ivy cursed, hating the loneliness of the night that stretched out before her like an ugly emptiness. She hated being alone. And she hungered for something more than mere raw sex with any man who happened to offer himself up for a night of fun and games.

Glen had helped to change all that and had become very important to her.

Damn him!

Hal Kenyon stepped from the men's room and spotted Ivy standing there, smoking and looking off into the distance. She saw him step up to her, smiling.

"Well, baby, you been two-timed?" he greeted, sounding pleased.

"Don't cut, Hal!" she snapped nastily back. "I'm

not in the mood!"

Hal's large face grew serious; his chiseled features seemed almost tender. He was a hugely built man with large, thick hands, and a broad well filled out chest. She had caught him in the past giving her the inviting eye, but it had always been a silent, passive flirtation.

Ivy dropped her cigarette butt, ground it into the floor with a pointed high-heel, and then asked: "Have another for me?"

Hal searched awkwardly into his jacket pocket. She took a cigarette that he quickly lighted. In the flare of the match, Hal's eyes looked bright and eager.

Ivy considered the man. He wasn't the kind to attempt to move in on another guy's woman; and especially the boss' woman.

"Have anything planned, Hal?" she impulsively inquired, having made up her mind that there wasn't any reason in the world she had to be alone. She didn't need to be alone!

Hal grinned a large toothy grin that made his rugged features almost look handsome. "Nothing at all."

"Neither do I, and I want company tonight!" she announced, grabbing his arm and squeezing. "What you say?"

His grin widened ever more as he gripped hold of her hand. "I say it's a great idea!" His eyes moved instinctively to her neckline, which revealed a generous amount of flesh. "What'd you have in mind?"

"A night lunch, with all the trimmings?" she offered, pressing her thigh. against his as they started out the back entrance of the club.

"Sounds interesting," Hal retorted in a husky voice.

"We could have something sent up to the room," Ivy suggested as they started down the back alley toward the street where Hal had parked his car. "And I have a bottle of—"

"I have a bottle, too, and have been wanting to share it with somebody!" Hal told her forcefully.

Ivy blinked, surprised. Hal had always been easygoing, kidding, quiet; it surprised her to hear such a strong statement from his lips.

Suddenly the idea of bedding down with Hal Kenyon took on new proportions of interest. In fact, Ivy realized, it was more than just interesting, it was intriguing. He was such a large man, such a hunk of male flesh. All at once Ivy felt a strange wildness excite her. Maybe things would be more interesting than she had thought.

Then she remembered Glen, who was with Lynn Bennings, and a stab of angry jealousy gnawed her.

She looked at Hal as he helped her into his '57 Ford, and tried to tear her thoughts away from Glen.

You have your own evening to enjoy—to hell with Glen and his little rich bitch! Ivy told herself. Almost immediately her mind shifted into second gear, cutting off the emotional side of her feelings and merely riding along the more sensual surface awareness. It was going to be kick night—a new kick—a new man—maybe a new kind of thrill!

Maybe that's where she needed to be!

The car pulled away from the corner and shot like a rocket down the street.

What soon followed was a real eye-opener to

Ivy. She really didn't expect that Hal would turn out to be such a great ball.

They literally knocked each other silly sexually. In many ways it had been brutal; though an exciting form of sexual bed games.

To Ivy it was good escape; to Hal it seemed a feast of pleasure for a starving man.

The all stayed at the same hotel, the rooms were functional and quite okay for a night lunch.

Ivy had undressed quite naturally before the man, while he poured stiff drinks of whiskey.

As she removed her bra, the man turned, saw the large lovely supply of breasts, his eyes growing large with immediate erotic interest.

That look, thrilled Ivy. She could almost feel his lips voluptuously sucking on her nipples. The thought and promise of this made her almost weak.

How she needed a man!

By the time she stood before him with only her white lace panties on, fingers tucked under the elastic band, Ivy grinned tauntingly.

"There's something here for you, you big hunk of male animal!" she promised, slowly peeling down the panties, inching them so that he had a prolonged sexual show. The expression on his face indicated just how much he was enjoying it.

Ivy felt like being all but raped. Ravished. Brutally taken. And Hal was the kind of guy who would willingly give her this kind of sexual service. She felt sure of it.

She was certain Hal would go for this kind of show tonight. "I got me a little somethin' hot for you!" she informed him, slowly revealing more and more of her naked flesh.

"Hell, Ivy, what's with you, tonight?" Hal choked out in a very husky voice. suddenly lowering the whiskey bottle to the dresser at his

"I want something wild and I sure the hell am going to try something real groovy for us tonight!" she announced, leaning over to step out of her panties. Her breasts were hanging down, their already hardened nipples like little points.

Hal said: "You got the hottest tits I've ever seen."

He stepped forward, reached out, as if to touch her, but Ivy backed gleefully away.

"Not yet, lover. Show me what you have to offer!" She cupped her breasts with the palms of her hands so that they were lifted up, the nipples extended forward. "Give me a peep show. Okay? And I'll let you suck my tits right off!"

He chuckled and unbuckled his belt, a second later his pants were open and lowered over his hips. Then he pushed down his shorts and Ivy gasped in pleasure.

"Is that what you wanted to see?" he countered with a proud grin.

"More than see, love. Why don't you get totally naked. Then I'll let you know everything I want to have."

"It better be more chit chat," he warned, beginning to step out of his slacks.

"Never fear, a lot of talking, but not in English."

"Then in what kind of language?"

Hal was now unbuttoning his shirt.

"French? Is that good enough?" she offered.

"Depends on where you are talking French," he laughed, pulling off his shirt.

"All over, you hot stud!" She was already almost trembling in excitement. The conversation alone was thrilling her in a highly erotic way. She was like that at times.

Hal leaned close, and pulled her into his arms, covering her lips with his. Their tongues met, hungrily.

The feel of his hairy chest against her nipples built the already driving heat of her body to a pressure point that was difficult to control.

"I'm so hot!" she moaned as the kiss broke.

By this time both of them were already driven beyond the point of control and suddenly he was crushing her against him.

Ivy said in a husky, panting voice: "Oh, I need it. Now, honey. All of you!"

It was one of those times when movement and action became blurred because of the overwhelming sensations driving through her body.

Ivy was never aware of anything other than the fact that suddenly Hal was on top of her. She was lying on her back, thighs spread wide, legs wrapped about his, holding him in a vise-like embrace.

"Hal, don't wait!" she almost screamed, clawing at his muscular back.

Frantically, Ivy thrust up and experienced the sensation her whole nervous system was screaming to know. From then on it was brutal and rapid. Neither wanted anything other than the selfish pleasure of quick orgasm.

Ivy sobbed. Time blurred in the sea of wonderful sensations bathing over her flesh. Then the world seemed to burst into nothing but fiery orgasm.

She heard him say: "Hell, Ivy, you're great."

When it was over the two of them were momentarily exhausted enough to lie side by side. How long they rested, Ivy didn't know, for it was difficult to tell for sure if she slept, since her state of mind was in that semi-conscious level where time is meaningless.

Later they showered together, continuing the sexual play.

Hal's power to continue responding to her matched her own desperate hunger,

She'd never known him to be like this before. Usually he was shyer, far less aggressive; now he was all over her at once.

As they stood in the shower, her back facing him, he embraced her so that his hands crushed against the swelling flesh of her breasts.

How it happened she wasn't quite sure. But somehow, even in the slippery dimension of the bathtub shower, she was bent over enough so that he suddenly thrust between her fanny cheeks and she became electrified with overwhelming pleasure as he penetrated her. The surprise of such union doubled Ivy's pleasure and she struggled to take totally possess him.

After that it was almost impossible to continue bathing, getting dry they collapsed on the bed.

They slept for a long time in each other's arms.

Later he made love to her again.

Hal was good; a tower of animal force. She could only guess that it was the build-up of a long silent waiting. No doubt the man had desired her for a long time and when the moment had finally become reality, he had exploded with the pent-up energy and physical longing.

She felt a sense of tenderness for the big bull of a man. Then she remembered Glen and his tenderness and the emotional feeling she experienced in his arms, and another type of sensation waved through her. She frowned, shivered.

Ivy reached for one of the stiff drinks Hal had poured for her and then gulped it down in one long swallow.

The liquor burned her throat and settled into the pit of her stomach like fiery acid. It took some moments before she felt the burning effects soothe over her brain.

As she stood there gazing almost impersonally at the man, Hal slowly lifted upwards, sat up, looked at Ivy. His eyes ran the full length of her body, burning bright with that expression all men have when looking at the nude form of a very sexy woman.

"You're beautiful!" he said after a moment, swinging his legs over the side of the bed and standing. Then he stepped over toward her and took the other glass, swallowing hard on the whiskey. His eyes fastened on her breasts, and an automatic lustful expression grew slowly there.

"You really have some breasts!" he admired, reaching out and caressing her.

Ivy laughed. "What late show did you hear that from?"

He merely smiled, then slid his arm around her waist, drawing her closer.

"I've wanted you for a long time, Ivy...a very long time," he announced in a husky voice.

Ivy looked into his eyes and felt suddenly sorry for the man. If he only knew the true direction of

91

her thoughts at that moment he wouldn't be so anxious to commit himself to her. All she could really think about was that Glen being with Lynn Bennings.

The man's lips covered hers and for that Ivy was suddenly glad. She pressed herself tight against him, opened her mouth to the kiss and felt a sensual stab as his tongue surged deep past her teeth.

At least she could literally feast on this big male body. The man found her hot, wanted her, and she wanted to simply escape in erotic sensations—and forget everything else.

Chapter Ten

Earl Bennings was sitting in the drawing room, nervously attempting to read a book that suddenly held no interest. Mercedes was playing the piano in the far corner of the room, seemingly not aware of his nervousness.

His eyes would track the words on the page, but no mental image would impress his brain.

Finally he slammed the book shut and then closed his eyes, resting his head on the back of the chair.

He'd had a hard but well spent life; a life that had actually centered around his wife and daughter. Nothing he had done had been for anybody else.

There were the years of the Twenties when he'd made deals to import illegal booze into the country—but that had been to create security for his child, his wife. He had grown up in a poor family, been given nothing to start with, had been forced to work up the hard way. And it had taken time before he'd been able to afford much more than a small room and a cheap suit of clothes. In those years Earl Bennings had worked as a strong arm man for a politically minded thug: but it had taught him something that had stayed with him for the rest of his life.

A guy had to fight hard to get ahead; had to fight in any means possible to take the next step. If somebody got hurt in the process, that was just too bad. People got hurt because they didn't have the guts to really fight for what they wanted. If you didn't hurt them somebody else would. The smart fellow hit first and picked up the rewards before some other slicker got there. You fought your way to the top.

And there had been a lot of women along the way. Most had been whores—in modern time called call-girls. He remembered how they would come in, take their money and ask what kind of party he wanted. He had several whom he hired time and again, each for a different purpose. If he wanted a blow-job he would call in a young girl who was really good at it. When it came to tit sucking, he knew one who had big boobs and large nipples. Sometimes he even hired two girls at once, who could give him a great time.

But usually he hired whores to keep business friends happy. There was one who really dug anal intercourse. Another who liked to have three women at once.

In big business it was always necessary to hire female flesh. Many deals had been made via a woman's body.

He knew too much about the way men could use a woman and what they thought of a girl who gave out to all and any comers.

For that reason alone he would have been very protective towards his daughter.

Just the idea of Lynn having sexual intercourse with a man made him sick inside, even though he realized that legally she was an adult and had the right to do anything she pleased.

But he'd kill rather than let her marry a man who just wanted to get rich quick.

So far murder hadn't been a part of his business.

One thing that Earl Bennings was glad about was that he'd never killed a man, or been responsible for a person's death even indirectly. He had moved in a tough circle, but managed to keep himself clean. After the depression he had managed to collect enough money to keep building, keep climbing, until by the mid-forties he was beginning to run Davis City. He was, to all practical purposes, the political boss of the county. Many mayors and congressmen owed their jobs—at one time or another—to his backing. At times it had been necessary to fight dirty. But he'd only been first, before others could beat him to it.

And all that for his wife and daughter. Especially for Lynn. He would do anything to assure Lynn's happiness. Anything he thought necessary— even if it might mean pushing so hard that somebody got really hurt, for good!

He didn't like the idea of Lynn getting involved with a jazz musician. Earl had seen and known too many, had watched their way of life, and knew the kind that was necessary for such people. Show business was exciting from the outside looking in, but in reality was a hectic, insane existence and only a few people could really be fully happy.

He especially hated jazz musicians. That was a very personal, hurtful, hatred that years had not dimmed nor dulled. He lived with it by ignoring the memories when they tried to surface.

Earl jerked up, stood, walked to the small bar

cabinet in the far corner. He poured himself a shot of expensive Scotch and then downed it in one gulp.

Mercedes stopped playing the piano, and said:

"What's wrong now?"

"I don't like it, Lynn taking up with the...trumpet player!" he growled, snapping his eyes in her direction.

She shrugged and looked very guarded. "You shouldn't take such a tight hold on Lynn. She's over twenty-one, and old enough to know what she wants out of life."

"Oh, shit! Don't hand me that! She's only a kid. What does she know about life? What does she know about this man—and she's fallen all over herself! I don't like it! And I'm going to do something about it when she gets home!" He looked at his watch. "God! It's past one. Where the hell is she?"

He frowned and then tapped his watch with a thick forefinger.

"Now, Earl—after all, she's not a teenager. Even if she stayed out all night, that's her business!"

"That's my business! I won't have any daughter of mine laying it with a crummy two-bit trumpet player. I won't have Lynn making a damned fool out of herself! Hell, you should know better … and understand—these guys are like bees, flitting from flower to flower! They grab their honey wherever they can get it, and then forget. No daughter of mine is going to become just another flower. I'll kill him!"

Mercedes stood, her face anguished with pain and anger.

"You've never forgiven me. Earl!" she said in a small voice.

96

"No! That's not it, and—"

"Yes it is, Earl. And you know it. Just because I made a fool of myself once, you can't forget—you think that all musicians are like that! You sometimes surprise me, Earl." She stepped across the room toward him and then came to a stop only inches away, looking up into his eyes. "Earl, that was a long time ago and a different time. I made a fool of myself because I was lonely—you'd been away in Washington with Henry for months—I was desperate. You know how I am about sex—I always needed it. It was as much your fault as mine—and his!"

"I don't want to talk about it!" Earl snapped angrily, twisting around and jerking out of room in choppy little steps. He went into his study and slammed the doors shut behind him, locking them. Then he slumped down onto the sofa.

His thoughts remembered that time some thirty years before, when he'd gone to Washington with Henry Yates, a young man who was anxiously attempting to get a seat in the House of Representatives. A lot of political pull, parties, promotion, the making of the right friends, finally put it through. But it had taken months—long months when he was away from Mercedes.

She had stayed home; then one night while visiting the club he'd owned then, she had started talking to a singer who was working for the club. How it had happened Earl had never really known. All he knew was that Mercedes had had an affair with the man. She'd followed him to the next city where he worked; she continued to follow the man until he gave her the brush. It had hurt her pride, and almost ruined their marriage. Only because Earl had felt guilty about one affair he'd had in Washington some years before was it possible for him to understand the situation and forgive his wife. That was the only time he'd come close to killing a man; Mercedes had talked him out of it.

Earl sat there thinking about the past, trying to honestly decide if that event could possibly have anything to do with his reaction to Lynn seeing Glen Fletcher. In the end he had to admit he didn't really know. Still he didn't like it at all!

When Lynn got home he would have a long talk with her, and make her see the light!

* * * * * * *

Mercedes was trapped in a mental well of her own thinking. Ever since Glen Fletcher had entered their lives she found her thoughts replaying those days with her own extramarital affair.

The man had been terribly good looking and the way he sang had almost given her an orgasm.

The first night when they climbed into bed together, she had felt terrible guilt but hadn't been able to control herself.

He made love in a wonderful way, thrillingly. Touching, caressing, kissing. Every time he penetrated her it was like some heavenly moment of pleasure that she'd never experienced with anyone before. Most of this was caused by her own loneliness.

Sometimes she wished it was possible to totally forget that experience, because she loved her husband and felt guilty about having cheated on him in that way; most of all, because it had given her so much sexual pleasure.

There wasn't anything she wouldn't do to please his sexual hungers and for the time the affair lasted it was a carnal feast almost without stop.

With her own husband, sex was always something special. But different. He was a good lover and a wonderful husband when it came to taking care of his wife. Yet at times she was almost afraid of him.

She was terrified of his attitude towards Lynn. If something wasn't done, the man would force their daughter into a life of frustration and unhappiness. Lynn deserved better.

Because of that Mercedes was determined to do everything possible to make sure Lynn married the man of her own picking. No matter what the cost might be.

If only Earl would understand how it was to be a woman and have human sexual needs and emotional hungers that only a man she loved could give.

*If only...*she thought.

MIDNIGHT LOVERS, BY CHARLES NUETZEL

Chapter Eleven

As Glen stepped into his hotel room behind Lynn he felt a strange sense of uneasiness. The place suddenly looked shabby and he was ashamed of it. He closed the door, then said awkwardly, "How about that drink?"

Lynn looked around the room, then glided over to the bed and sat down, feeling the softness.

"Well, a hotel room is a hotel room!" she grinned.

He poured their drinks and then sat down next to her on the bed. The hot need had burst so freely a few moments before in the car now had simmered down slightly and he didn't know exactly how to approach the subject again. He handed her a drink and then took a strong sip of his own.

Suddenly Glen felt like a little inexperienced child who has never had a woman before. And in a way there was a little bit of truth to that feeling. It was different with Lynn than it had been with all the other women he had taken to his hotel rooms during the past years. The difference was unsettling, especially since he realized that there really couldn't be that much difference. Lynn was fully mature, adult; she had come to his hotel room because she desired to become intimate with him. He didn't doubt that she'd been in bed with other men in the past. Yet he felt unsure of himself, unable to decide on the right moves to make or when to make them. Maybe, he told himself, it was because he cared so damned much; because he wanted everything to be perfect. With other broads it was just for kicks and it didn't really matter what they thought. They'd up to have sex with the celebrity and that was it. He'd given them what they wanted. What made him think that Lynn was really any different from them? A young rich girl who had a crush on the trumpet player— how could that be different?

Annoyed, Glen stood, finished off his drink, went to the dresser where the bottle of whiskey sat, and then poured himself another stiff shot. He turned to find Lynn's eyes on him.

She was smiling, but the light in her eyes was hesitant, almost frightened.

He wanted to tell her this was all a mistake; he wanted to say he desired her body, her emotions, her love, but didn't want to do it this way, this time. He had so many things he wanted to say, but the words merely choked in his throat and wouldn't come out.

She sat there for a moment longer and then suddenly put down her glass and started unbuttoning her dress.

Glen stood there, frozen, hardly able to breathe as he watched Lynn removing her clothing. Finally she stood and reached around to the back of her bra. She hesitated for only a moment and then released the clasp.

She looked magnificent. Her hips were rounded and beautiful, her flesh creamy, flawless, her breasts

102

well-formed cups of flesh, and as they were freed of the confining bound of the bra they relaxed, but merely surged outwards, rather than down. They were perfectly shaped, dotted with rosy beacons that seemed to silently call to him.

She stood there for a few moments as if attempting to decide whether she should remove her panties or not, then seemed to have decided against it. With one graceful move, she slipped under the covers of the bed and waited for him.

There wasn't any turning back now, and for that Glen was thankful. The sight of her naked breasts had excited him to a point of not wanting to turn back. She had made the plunge, as if guessing his hesitation. In a way it was her show from here on.

Still Glen hesitated. He wondered if once he possessed her it would end the spell, finish his emotional desires for Lynn. Could it be that he only really desired her body, and wanted to live out the fantasy of love as long as possible? Was that what bothered him?

Gently putting down the now empty glass, Glen stepped to the bed. He sat down beside Lynn, taking in the perfection of her face that rested so beautifully against the pillow.

Is this really what you want, Lynn? he mentally asked her. But of course she didn't answer because she hadn't heard the question.

She merely smiled up at him and then reached out her arms, very womanly and at the same time very child-like.

And at the moment Glen felt all the emotions that a man might feel toward the woman he loves. The emotions flooded up over him, drowning all other thoughts, filling him completely.

"Oh, Lynn," he moaned, slipping down beside her, kissing her throat, her ear, running his lips along the shadow of her silken hair, kissing her eyes, as if they were the most valuable things in the world. And with every kiss, every touch, the emotion swelled up in him like a fiery ache that held him frozen in its power.

"Lynn," he breathed again, covering her lips with his own. Her hands caressed the back of his neck, her lips opened and he dipped into the rich wine of her mouth.

It was an all-embracing kiss, the kind that used every nerve and every emotion in him; a tenderness, a gentle moment of love that captured him completely.

Then slowly he slipped away and stood, carefully removing his clothing, all the time watching her, experiencing the love emotion even stronger than before.

It wasn't hard to love such a woman; yet he couldn't understand how it could have happened so fast, how it could have become so powerful. Surely once he had possessed her it would all be different; he would be able to see what she really meant to him—and it couldn't be all of this! All the wonderful feeling which now was in complete possession of him.

As he slipped down to the bed, Lynn pulled covers away from her body.

They slid together, embraced tenderly. She hugged to him like a little child. They kissed and it was heaven in the shape of a woman. Rich wine, pouring through his veins. He was riding a fleecy

104

cloud of yellow-gold, a heaven-soaring cloud that raced higher and higher upwards.

The soft warmth of her flesh against his slowly created its spell through him. The supple pressure of her breasts cushioned against his chest like silken cushions.

He kissed her again, caressingly; then his hand found her body, lightly brushed over the softness of her. She trembled against him and her lips hungrily convulsed against his.

"Oh, Glen," she murmured a moment later as he moved his kiss along her shoulder and to the shape of her breasts. "I love you...oh, I love you!"

But he hardly heard the words, for his mind was only centered on his own emotional response to this woman who had come so quickly and completely into his lonely life.

He wanted to make love to every inch of her; he wanted to touch, caress, kiss all there was of her wonderful body. He wanted to embrace her in his arms forever, tenderly, and lovingly.

The kisses became more intimate, more exciting, and the emotion swelled, mixing with the physical need that her nearness created. She writhed under his kisses. And it continued for what seemed a lovely eternity of touches, caressing surrender to one another. Her own hands played along his back, over his shoulders and then gripped hard as their bodies joined in the final moments of the love-making.

He felt himself slowly whipped upwards, high, like a soaring rocket shooting into the blackness of space, into the Mardi Gras of stars that twinkled happily at him.

And afterwards he fell slowly down toward the reality of the world, back into the small hotel room in which he had found love for the first time in too many years.

He lay there next to her, holding the woman in his arms, caressing her hair, loving her as much, if not more than he had before.

He wanted to draw her to him, in soft tenderness, embrace all of her in one delicious union after another. He wanted to fold himself around and as she folder him into her. I wanted to protect this soft, delicate, lovely women, to be a shield of strength and power, to be everything a man might be to the woman he love and treasured beyond all others.

It was a new experience sensing these things; for usually all his sexual activities had been mostly for orgasm, nothing more.

But when he'd loved her breasts, pulled those pink, firm nipples between his lips, it had been a different sexual act; a love act. He had simply wanted to give pleasure, to worship her as if she were some kind of goddess, some wonderful perfection. He wanted to let her know how much she meant to him. He had never wanted to give so fully to anybody in his life. It was overwhelming.

When his hands had discovered the heat of her and his lips had followed, the welling thrill of giving pleasure had been greater than the need of taking it.

And that made all the difference in the world.

* * * * * * *

Lynn, for her own part, was overwhelmed by

the experience of being made love to by this man.

She wanted to cry with joy.

Then suddenly she was clawing all over her lover, arousing him, wanting to know and give the pleasure they had just experienced.

Suddenly she was straddling his hips, leaning over him, gasping in passionate desire, feeling the powerful hardness of him so wonderfully within her grasp. She couldn't stop sobbing, driving at him, with such wildness that it made her almost choke in pleasure. Then later, it was slowly given and taken, and she was riding on some wonderful cloud, must moaning softly, just sighing as they rode together over one wave after another, bathing across their bodies, uniting them in a unified act of total love that enveloped all of their beings. It was as if their souls had merged and fused into one unified being.

From that moment on she couldn't get enough; she never wanted to stop.

When climax came for both of them it was electrically overwhelming to the point where they fell against one another, clutching in their exhausted pleasure.

Chapter Twelve

How long they lay there, he didn't know. But suddenly the decision was made for him—a decision which had to be made fast or not at all.

He sat partly up, looked down into Lynn's eyes, and said in a soft, almost frightened voice:

"Lynn...would you think it was wrong if I asked you to marry me?"

It seemed forever before she said anything. She just lay there, her expression unchanged for what couldn't have been more than an instant, but was all of life to Glen.

"Oh, Glen, do you really mean it?" she cried, flinging her arms about his neck, drawing herself tightly against him. "Really, honestly mean it?"

Glen choked on his own words, stammering them out like a school kid. "I...mean...it so much. It's so fast. But...but I never...never met any-body...any woman...like you before."

And it was so terribly true. Everything he had wanted in a woman was in this woman in his arms. There wasn't any doubt or hesitation about accepting that fact. Tenderness, intelligence, strength, and yet that child-like quality that so appealed to him. Yet she was all woman, so much woman!

"I know, Lynn," he managed in a more even voice, "that this is all so sudden—and we hardly know each other. But how much can a person know another until they live together? We know as much as we could ever know! I love you. I love everything about you! No matter what that might be. There isn't anything about you that is false or horrid, that I couldn't love with my very soul. This love has the truth about it…conviction…totality. Just like when you blow a perfect chorus, a jazz riff that blends with the heavens and you know it is perfect, you know it is right, you understand without logic or reason that you have created something so … sometimes it just happens. And when it does there is no doubt about it. And that's what has happened to me with you. I want you in my life forever."

She drew silently away, her face frowning. For a moment she didn't say anything. Then, as if afraid, as if frightened to even say it, she said:

"Glen, you aren't trying…trying to get at…my father's…"

"Money! To hell with money. No wife of mine works, or has any money other than what I make. If you can accept that, then we're in! I want you for what you are. Nothing more! Just you!"

She smiled, said: "I've loved you from the moment I saw you, and it's never changed."

She hugged tighter to him.

"It won't be an easy life. Lynn. I'll be on the road for lot of time…"

"Aren't other musicians married?" she pointed out. "Don't their wives go along?"

"Of course, but I just—"

"But nothing!" She put a delicate finger on his

110

lips. Glen was dazed by what was happening, but felt no doubt about it being completely right.

Then thought of Lynn's father caused a shiver to rush over him.

"What's wrong?" Lynn asked.

"Your father. What about him? I have a feeling he might be a problem. Is he?"

She frowned, her lips pursed up tight, dimpling at the corners. "We'll have to tell him. Please… don't let him…change things."

"We could get married right away. Drive over the state line and—"

Lynn shook her head. "Not that way, Glen. Not unless we have to. Dad would never forgive me. Never. I couldn't do that—unless it was the only way!"

Suddenly they were in each other's arms again. They held close, clutching like two lost children. It was a long time before the desperation of their situation smothered out to be replaced by the intimate closeness of their naked bodies.

All at once Glen was aware of his erection pressing against Lynn's stomach and she revealed her own sense of growing need by squirming slightly.

It was all the communication required. Each of them needed escape from the fear of loosing one another. They needed the reassurance of one another's love, body, union.

Yet there was so much he wanted to say. The words tumbled out as he breathed against her stomach: "Oh, God, I love you!"

All at once he was smothered against her breasts and her thighs were parted wide in open invitation to his total love-making.

"Oh, I love you, Glen!" she told him in a deeply passionate voice. "Oh, love me like forever…as if it might never happen again. Oh love—"

She broke off with a gasp as her legs locked about his body. They moved like two savage animals in perfect rhythm, not stopping in their furious need to become one being until mutual orgasm shuddered through their bodies.

Even then Lynn wouldn't release her grip, wouldn't relax her hold upon his body.

And suddenly he realized how powerful their love for one another must be, how great their sexual feelings and needs match.

"Lynn, dear, dear Lynn," he breathed against her lips. And he murmured words of love over and over to her, as if he couldn't exhaust the expression of them, couldn't flood her with enough such verbal caresses. Then the words became actions and they were united in another loving embrace that just kept building within them until they couldn't stop.

Suddenly Lynn was laughing in delight and caressing his shoulders.

They both stared into each other's eyes, taking in the sight of deeply felt ecstasy they were giving one another.

Afterwards, bathed in sweat, panting in the aftermath of their union of total love, they were silent for a very long time. Finally they slid apart. Shortly after that Lynn slipped from the bed, stood, moved to her clothing.

"You'd better take me home. I'll tell Dad when it's the best time."

She hesitated, adding: "That is…if you still—"

"Quiet, my dear love. It will never change with me. Mad though it is, I love you forever!"

She smiled, then was serious looking. "I hope you feel the same after Dad works his nasty on you!"

"Nothing will change how I feel, Lynn," he assured her.

But Glen couldn't help feeling there would be a rough road ahead. If he had only guessed, then, how rough it would be, he might have pushed the issue of a secret marriage. But nobody can tell what the future will bring—and so he merely nodded, stood and began dressing.

"You best take me home, so I can tell dad…best I do it alone. I know him."

When he started to protest she shook her head, determined: "If you really want to marry me, if you really love me, you'll have to learn to trust me. I know dad. I know what is best. Believe me, Glen. Let me handle this."

He considered, the shrugged. "So…I'll drive you home."

* * * * * * *

Lynn stepped down the hallway, tiptoeing, hoping to slip by her father's study, in which she could see a light through the crack of the door.

As she started past, the doors opened and Earl Bennings stormed out.

"Well, hello!" he greeted, silkily, in the way that told Lynn all too clearly that he wasn't in a good mood.

"Hi, Dad," she said, lightly.

"Will you come on in?" he offered, making a motion toward the study.

"Right now, Dad? I'm tired and—" She wanted to talk to him, she wanted to be done with this part, but also wanted a few moments alone, to form the right words to let him know about her coming marriage to Glenn.

"Now!" he exclaimed.

She studied his face and saw the hardness in his narrowed eyes. A shiver shot over her. How she loved her father—but how she feared him too.

"Okay, Dad, we might as well get it over with right now!"

She walked into the room, and the doors closed noisily behind her. Earl Bennings was silent for a long time, then he said: "I understand you were out with the trumpet man."

"With Glen," she said boldly, standing straight and challenging him with her eyes.

"Oh, so you want to play it that way," he told her. "Okay. Lynn, I don't like this. A crush is one thing...anything else, I won't put up with!"

Lynn felt a fury build up in her. "Father, look. I'm old enough to know my own mind, and you and nobody else is going to tell me how to live my life, or who I'll see! Do you understand?"

They glared at one another for a moment, then Earl Bennings stepped closer, put his hands on her shoulders, smiled and said: "Darling, don't you know I have your best interests at heart? I love you very much. But I understand about life a little more than you do. You're everything to me. You and your mother," he quickly added. "Everything I've done has been for the women in my life—you and your

114

mother. I don't want you ruining your future by getting involved with the wrong kind of man and—"

"What would be the right kind of man?"

"When he comes along, I'll know!"

"I don't think you do know, or ever will know! Nobody will be good enough for your daughter. You'll have me an old maid. Look, I'll live my own life—and you keep out of it!"

Earl's face clouded. "I don't want you seeing this...Glen Fletcher any more! That's final!"

Lynn suddenly laughed. It was a high, bitter sound; mocking. "I'm afraid you can't stop it!"

"Oh, you don't think so?" he cried. Then more softly, "Look, Lynn. I know men like this guy. They take a woman's body and when they've had it, that's the end! They aren't interested any more and—"

Lynn blurted out, without thinking, "I've slept with him—and we're getting married!"

Earl Bennings' face looked as if it had been slapped. He blinked, the features grew tight, drained. Slowly he stepped back, his mouth opened as if to say something. Then it snapped shut.

For a moment longer he stood there, then he moved to the large leather chair and slumped down onto it.

"You...you must...be kidding!" he stammered, not looking at her.

"I'm not. We would have run across the state line and gotten married, but I wanted to let you know in the right way and the right time and . . well, I didn't think it was fair to you or Mother to go off and sneak that way. Now either you accept it, or we do what's necessary. I'm in love with him—and he's in love with me—and that's the way it stands. There isn't a thing in the world you can do to change that!"

Earl Bennings slowly stood, turned, faced his daughter and said: "Lynn, there is a lot I can do. Just like I've done in the past! Money talks. And believe me, your little trumpet player isn't any different from any other man who wanted to marry you!"

Lyn started to say something to that, but decided against it. Maybe it would be good for all concerned to let her father play out his little act. When Glen turned him flat down, it would be impressive.

She turned and stepped to the door. Just before leaving, she said: "You're in for a shock! I hope you won't be too disappointed."

As she left, her father's last words rang in her ears like knives: "I won't!"

Chapter Thirteen

Glen was sleeping when there was a knock on his hotel room door. For a moment he felt a sense of confusion, because he'd been dreaming about Lynn, about their future together. It had been difficult letting her go home alone, without him at her side; it had been a nightmare struggle to kiss her goodbye and watch her leave. It was as if he were losing the only thing of value in his life. Then he convinced himself that things would be all right. After all, she knew her father. She wasn't stupid. And he trusted her. He had to. Getting to sleep had been difficult, but the dreams had been a delicious replay of their hours together. Then suddenly he was awake.

As the knocking continued, he slowly slipped out of bed and then gathered his morning robe.

"Hold on," he shouted.

The pounding stopped short.

Pulling the robe around him, Glen stepped to the door and flung it open. For a moment he was too dazed to react.

Standing there was Earl Bennings. The man's face was tired and tight-looking; there was a redness around his eyes, and the drooping expression on his set mouth accented the appearance of hardness.

"Oh, come on in." Glen offered, smiling his most winning smile. He closed the door behind the man. "Well, quite a surprise. I wasn't expecting you."

Bennings merely made a grunting sound behind his tightly clamped teeth. He looked at Glen for a long, stony moment and then reached into his jacket pocket. Pulling out his wallet, he extracted what looked like a check from it.

"Well, boy, I understand you've been playing up to my daughter." His voice was as hard as his eyes. "I can quite understand your motives, all things considered."

He swept the room with his right hand and shrugged. "Now, I can understand your position—after all, I was young one time and I had dreams and visions.

"But we must be intelligent about this. And I plan on playing this fair. I've arranged things so that you don't have to worry about staying in town any longer—and here's my check for ten thousand dollars, so you won't feel too much put out!" He extended the check. "I'm certain you fully understand what I'm saying. And why."

Glen stood there, amazed, unable to believe what was taking place. For a long time he couldn't think of anything to say, but the fury was building up in him like the pressure of a volcano that is about to explode.

"Oh, don't be so surprised. I admit the money is rather...let's say it's a lot for your short investment. But I love my daughter, and I'll do anything necessary to see that she gets the best out of life!" He pushed the check into Glen's relaxed hand. "Here, take it!"

Glen grabbed hold of the check, crumpled it in his hands and then let it fall to the floor.

"Now," he said, "that this end of the business is over with, let's have an understanding. I won't—*shut up!*" he yelled, as the older man was about to say something. "I won't be bought off. I'm not interested in your money—or your daughter's money! I make a good living, and I'm climbing upwards! I have a good future. I love your daughter and she loves me, and we're going to be married, regardless of what you try to do to stop us, and—"

"Boy, quiet!" Earl snapped in a low, tense, dangerous voice. "I've listened enough. There is no reason to continue. You either cash that check or tear it up—I don't care which. But you won't see my daughter again—ever! You won't work in this town again! And if you try to get in my way again, you won't work anywhere!"

The man attempted to leave the room, tried to get past Glen, but Glen grabbed hold of his shoulder.

"Who the hell do you think you are?" Glen spat out, holding back the automatic desire to beat the hell out of the older man. "You can't run your daughter's life, and you can't run mine! She's old enough to do what she wants with her life. I'm not leading her into poverty, and I'm not about to hurt her! I love her—and everything goes with that!"

"What kind of life would you give her?"

"The kind she wants!"

"What do you know about Lynn? What in the world do you know about her? You slept with her—and for that I could kill you, and get away with it!"

119

Bennings warned. "You're lucky that I don't have you worked over good! Now take my advice and cash that check and get out of town before something serious happens you'll be sorry about for the rest of your life!"

Bennings jerked away from Glen and then swung open the door. He turned and looked at him just long enough to warn: "Leave town—or I'll fix you up real good!"

With that, Bennings slammed the door.

Glen stood there for a moment and then walked to the hotel phone, picked it up and asked for the Bennings' phone number.

"Put a call through."

When a man's voice answered the phone, Glen said, "Let me speak to Lynn Bennings."

"Who is this, sir?"

"Glen Fletcher."

"I'm sorry, but she's not in and—"

"Glen!" Lynn's voice sounded over the receiver. "Oh, I'm so glad to hear from you. Dad is furious and plans on paying you off and—"

"He was here. Get some things packed. We'll leave town immediately. Meet me—where we parked last night before coming here."

"Where we parked?" she inquired in a shaking, happy sounding voice.

"I'll be there in less than twenty minutes!" she announced.

"I love you," Glen said. "I love you too, darling!" A moment later the line was dead. Glen moved fast. First he called his agent, Monica Hall, and told her what had happened about the club engagement.

She said: "I just got a call from the manager. Okay—I can book you in for a week in Vegas. There's an opening there. Can you make it by night after tomorrow?"

"Think so."

"Fine. I'll call Vern in Vegas and let him know."

"How's the record project going?" Glen asked.

"Okay—maybe sign a contract in a couple of weeks, then you can either run into Los Angeles, or possibly do something live in Vegas. That'll work out...from the other end. I'll keep you informed."

They both said good-bye and then Glen called Ivy on the hotel phone. He asked her to come over to his room. Then he got Hal Kenyon's room on the phone.

"Hal, we're splitting town. Engagement's off."

"What happened?" the man boomed over the phone.

"Tell you later. Need a best man. Tell the other guys that..."

"What the hell? A best man—for what?"

"A wedding. I'm crossing over to Nevada. We're getting married there and—"

"Who?"

Just then the door opened and Ivy stepped in, closing the door behind her.

"I'll tell you later, Hal. Tell the other boys to make plans for Vegas. I'll see them at the Harvard Hotel in a couple of days. Okay?"

"Okay. When do you want me?"

"In about ten minutes."

"Short order."

"Quick arrangements!"

He hung up without saying good-bye, then turned to Ivy. He dreaded this next few moments. It wouldn't be easy, but it was only fair to tell her himself.

"Well?" she asked in a small voice, leaning against the door.

"I'm getting married," he blurted, realizing that the direct approach would be best.

She stood there for a long moment, not saying anything. Then her breasts heaved and she opened her mouth. A low sound preceded her first words. "You can't be serious."

"To Lynn. It happened! I don't know how—but just like that. I only hope you can understand, Ivy. I know what—"

"I don't want to hear any more, Glen!" she snapped. For a moment longer she stood there and then turned, flung the door open, and said: "I hope the...best!"

But her voice was choked, filled with emotion. She walked down the hall, and he listened to her quick footsteps disappearing into the distance.

Glen stood for a moment without moving, feeling momentarily sick inside, because a lot had happened between Ivy and himself, and he hated hurting her in this way. But it had been impossible to avoid. Finally he told himself that Ivy would get over it; that she would in time find another guy to sleep with—that she wasn't really the marrying kind.

Slowly Glen moved to gather up his clothing. It took a little less than five minutes to throw his things into the well worn suitcase, then he was just starting for the door when Hal stepped in, his face

122

puzzled.

"I'll tell you all about it on our way out of town. Okay?"

"Use your car."

"Yes. Have one of the boys drive yours."

Hal nodded.

They had sat in the restaurant for a little over ten minutes when Lynn Bennings arrived.

Glen stood the moment he saw her step out of the Ford she had been driving. Leaving the restaurant, he rushed up to her.

"I love you," he said, pulling her into his arms.

"Glen...everybody will see you!"

"Let them!"

She pushed away, out of his embrace, and said: "We'd better get out of here before Dad starts after us. I—"

Lynn suddenly broke off, her face contorted in horror.

"God !" she cried.

A car had just pulled into the parking lot. It shot toward them and then slammed to a stop.

Two men got out of the front seat; another, heavier one, groaned out of the back seat. He was Earl Bennings.

The two other men, large and brutish looking, stepped forward, followed by Bennings.

Glen said: "Look, let's be intelligent about this!"

His eyes were on the two men who had come to a stop only a few feet in front of them. Earl Bennings was already lumbering between them. He stepped up to Glen, his eyes hot and angry.

"Okay, boy. I tried to warn you and now—now

you're going to be very sorry!" he threatened. "One last chance. Then I turn you over to…these two men."

Glen could hardly believe what he was hearing. There they were in broad daylight, in the middle of an American town, and Earl Bennings was threatening him openly. It didn't seem possible that the man could actually carry out any threat, but it still amazed Glen to hear the words.

Hal Kenyon suddenly stepped up beside Glen.

"What's the trouble?" the large bass-man questioned, seeming to take the situation in one quick glance.

"Nothing we can't handle," Glen assured him, feeling suddenly more reassured to have a friend at his side, especially one as powerfully built as Hal.

Bennings grinned, said: "Look, boy, you might think I'm bluffing. Just simmer down and listen to an old man's advice."

Lynn spoke up suddenly. "Please, Dad, call off the twins—and let us go in peace." Her voice was angry, but still on the verge of tears. "I want to lead my own life, for once. I want my kind of happiness, not what you think is good for me, and—"

"Shut up, girl!" he snapped nastily. "Get in my car! That's an order!"

Lynn merely stood there, unmoving, glaring at her father, tight lipped. She leaned only slightly closer to Glen, as if for silent protection. Glen put an arm around her shoulder.

"Lynn!" Earl cried, taking a step toward his daughter. "Get in that car, immediately!"

Lynn trembled against Glen.

Glen said, "Come on, Lynn. Let's get out of

here! He wouldn't dare do anything!"

Glen started to step around the man, but Earl Bennings suddenly and without warning swung a hard right into Glen's face. It was a staggering, un-expected blow, which knocked him back, away from Lynn, stumbling against Hal.

"Get in the car!" Bennings ordered his daughter. "Get in there before it's too late."

Glen was dazed, his face throbbing where the older man's fist had hit him. He was about to leap forward to attack Bennings when Hal gripped hold of him.

The two thugs stepped between Bennings and Glen; stood there like two tall giants, dangerous and threatening.

Suddenly Bennings swung a blow across Lynn's face. "Now, get in the car!"

Glen saw red, ripping out of Hal's grip and leap-ing toward Bennings, right through the two man barrier that stood in his way.

The two thugs moved swiftly, surely. It was al-most a study in grace and speed. They worked like a well oiled machine.

Glen felt something grab hold of his arm, twist him around, grab his other arm, and swiftly pinned then behind his back, so fast that he couldn't even resist. Then a quick series of agonizing blows rammed at him like rapid fire hammers. He felt them like a continued flash of pain. One in his stomach, another in his face, and a third and fourth at his chest and side, then a fifth impact of pain in his groin.

A yell sounded. He felt the man who had been hitting him knocked away. Glen tired to regain his senses, attempted to gather the strength of his muscles, but couldn't. He was almost paralyzed in agony that rippled all over him, burning from nerve to nerve. The world was spinning, a distant red and a fading series of screams and grunts.

Then everything clouded around him and he was aware of nothingness, gentle nothingness that floated through every nerve, soothing away the pain until even thoughts blurred and melted away.

Chapter Fourteen

Ivy was taking a shower and finding her thoughts remembering the last time with Hal Kenyon. He had been strangely fantastic.

She thought how wonderful it would be to have Hal in the shower right then.

Or Glen.

That last realization puzzled her. Sex was one thing and the emotional thing something else.

Right at this moment she wished both men were with her.

It was in this mood that she got out of the shower and dried herself. She had just finished getting dressed when the phone rang. Hal's voice over the phone immediately killed all thoughts of inviting him over for a night lunch.

"Glen's been hurt. You better get a doctor and come right out yourself. We're at the out of town hash house," he said, knowing she would know what he meant. "Hurry, for God's sake. That bastard just left us here!"

Ivy didn't take the time to even bother asking exactly what happened. She quickly hung up the phone and then got the hotel clerk on the phone, asked for a doctor and then told the man where to send him.

The drive out to the restaurant was an agony for Ivy. All she could think of was that Glen had been hurt: she didn't know how badly and the thought of anything serious happening had overshadowed her earlier anguish about his marrying another woman.

Hal was standing next to an ambulance that had arrived a little before her.

The minute she got out of the car she saw his face was a mass of blood. Hal grinned crookedly at seeing her.

"Oh, Hal! What happened?" she cried, rushing up to him.

Then she saw Glen, who had just been put on a stretcher. His face looked horrible. The nose must have been broken, and both his eyes were swollen. The cut and bloody shape of his lips was all too re-vealing. Whoever had done this had tried to make sure he wouldn't play trumpet for a while.

A horror-filled gasp choked from her mouth at the sight, and she swayed. Hal caught her just in time.

"He'll be all right. You got good results. They arrived only a minute ago. But the doctor said that the damage wasn't too serious."

After a moment Ivy gained control of herself. "What happened?"

"Old Man Bennings didn't like the idea of his daughter taking up with Glen. He came storming up, and this was what happened afterwards."

"You must be kidding!" Ivy cried, unable to be-lieve this could happen.

Hal shrugged. "I'm riding with Glen. Want to come along, or follow in the car?"

128

Ivy nodded. "I'll ride along."

* * * * * * *

Lynn Bennings was pushed into her room by her father, who came in after her, slamming the door.

She was still under shock at what she had seen happen. But now, alone with her father, the fury ate its way up to the surface.

"I'm leaving, Dad...and there's nothing you can do about that!" she told him.

He merely smiled; a sure, almost oily smile. "Of course, darling. On the first plane to Germany—with me and your mother! I think a trip would be the best thing for you and—"

"What in the Goddamned hell makes you think you can make me go with you?" she fairly screamed at him.

"Lynn, I know you must hate me right now, but in time you'll be thanking God that I did. I did it for you—I did it because I can't stand by and see a daughter of mine make a fool of herself and ruin her life!"

"I'm old enough to do with my life what I want. So, please, leave me alone!" she cried, turning and falling on the bed. Tears rushed into her eyes, and suddenly she felt terribly alone, frightened and trapped.

"You'll thank God, Lynn!" Earl Bennings announced, as he opened the door. She heard him step out and then the door closed and there was a clicking sound. Without getting up Lynn knew she was locked in.

There was only one way out of the room, and

that was through the window and down one floor to the ground, without any means of getting there. She suddenly sat up, looked at her bed.

The sheets could possibly do the job.

Lynn moved to the window, looked down, and then her heart sank. There stood Vern Gordon, one of her father's strong arm men.

For the first time Lynn was seeing her father for what he was, and even that didn't really mean anything to her. Strangely it was as if she had known it all along but refused to admit it, and now was glad to face the truth.

What ever feelings were left for her father would be dead if he won this battle. That might be a lever on her side. The man could go just so far without losing her completely. He might not know it yet, but soon he would discover the price he could pay for trying to dominant her.

She would have her life, and the man she loved.

Somehow she had to get out of the house; somehow she had to find Glen and get away from this town, this state, and beyond her father's power to hurt them.

All her life seemed to flash before her eyes. All the lovers who didn't mean anything.

Now it was Glen. And he meant everything to her. And if she was wrong about him, then she'd face that on her own two feet. And she couldn't really imagine anything other than the truth of their love for one another.

He was the only one she cared about. The only human being that made life worth living. And because of her father...

Now her father was trying to take what little real

happiness she could possibly have away.

He was a selfish, demanding, cruel man.

Suddenly Lynn didn't know if she hated her father or not.

She hated what he was doing.

She loved Glen.

Why couldn't her father understand that?

A shudder raced over her body.

Lynn sat up, wondering what she really would do. If she couldn't have Glen, life didn't seem worth living.

If only there was somebody she could talk to. If only there were some escape from her father's clutches.

She'd give anything to be free. Now she realized what kind of prisoner she'd been all these years. A total slave to her father's whim.

Sobs of desperation and helplessness choked Lynn's throat and she fell back on the bed, crying uncontrollably.

* * * * * * *

When Mercedes Bennings heard what had happened she was at first horrified, then disgusted. All her life she had known what kind of man Earl was; had known that he would do anything to get his way, and would do anything to run his daughter's life.

"You can't do this!" she told him as they stood in the living room, glaring at one another.

"Who's going to stop me?" Bennings asked in a tough voice.

"I will!"

The man merely smiled tenderly at her. "Mercedes—don't you think I know what I'm doing?
I've worked hard, and I'm not going to have it all
thrown away on a man like this son-of-a-bitch bastard named Fletcher!"

Her thoughts fired, flared in fury. For a moment
she just couldn't think of anything to say that would
make her husband understand how cruel and wrong
he was.

If only she'd never had that affair years before.
If only she had been able to control herself. If this
man who called himself a husband and father had
been at her side when she needed him, things would
be so different now.

If only…

All the anguish of years flooded up through her
mind and body now as she looked at the man who
had been her husband and lover.

"You think I don't know what I'm doing? I've
worked hard, and I'm not going to have it all thrown
away on a man like this Fletcher!"

Mercedes felt suddenly sick inside. "Why do
you have to take it out on her? Take it out on me!"

"I'm not taking anything out on anybody! The
issue is closed. Finished. I warned that man and he
merely got what he asked for. Nothing more. He
was about to attack me—the boys merely stopped
him."

Mercedes looked at her husband for a moment
and then decided there was only one way to handle
the situation. Later, after it was dark, she would see
to it that Lynn had her chance to get away. She
wasn't about to stand quietly by and watch her
daughter's life ruined by a man who had become

132

bitter and hateful in his older age. Earl couldn't forget something that had happened too many years ago. He was filled with too much hate surrounding his hurt feelings.

"Okay, I guess you know what you're doing," she finally said in a mild voice. "I just hope you do!"

"I do, believe me. It's for the best of all concerned. We'll leave for Europe tomorrow morning. Get the things ready, and I'll arrange for tickets."

Mercedes left the room and then went up to her own private bedroom, which she had had for the last ten years. Life with Earl Bennings had never been an easy one. Oh, they had been in love, and continued to stay in love. But times, years, situations had changed a lot in their relationship. Sex had been a now and then thing, when both of them were able to forget the hurts of the past. A couple of times she'd been tempted to step out on Earl—but only that one time, many years ago, had marred her almost perfect record.

She thought about the young man whom Lynn was taken with, and she saw herself when she'd been young and in love with a man much like him. But there was a difference between them. Mercedes had learned a lot about people in her life, and was convinced that Glen Fletcher wasn't the kind who would say one thing and mean something different. She couldn't help thinking that Glen could be right for her daughter. And beyond that point, she honestly felt that Lynn had the right to live her own life.

That one pass she'd made at Glen at her birthday party had been a mere test, an attempt to see actually what kind of a man he was. It had been crude, but to her mind necessary. She'd do anything for her daughter; much like Earl.

But, Mercedes thought, *less selfishly.*

Mercedes picked up her private phone and dialed the city hospital.

"Let me speak to Doctor Winters," she said when the operator answered the call. There were only a few moments of waiting, then a husky, rasping voice spoke through the receiver.

"Ben," Mercedes said, "this is Mrs. Bennings. I wonder if you could do me a favor."

"Oh, anything!" the man exclaimed.

"There's a young man who was brought into your hospital a little while ago. Glen Fletcher. He was worked over by some—well, men. I wanted to know how he was."

"I'll check. I think Dr. Peters is working on the case."

There was a long, long wait until his voice sounded through the receiver again.

"Your boy is okay, from what I'm told. Peters said he would be up and around in a day or two—in fact, once he's patched up, he could be on his feet then. Just visual damage, but nothing serious."

"Could I speak to him?" she suddenly asked, a plan beginning to form in her mind.

"Not right now—he's still being worked on. Conscious, though. I could have a call put through for you when he's ready."

"I wish you would!"

* * * * * * *

Glen hurt all over. At least it seemed that way.

134

But the physical pain wasn't as deep as the emotional one.

Where would it end, now? he wondered as the doctor put the last bandage on his face.

The idea of living the kind of life he had in the past years created such an emotional anguish that Glen felt it wasn't worth considering.

He'd never felt this way about any woman before in his life. Without Lynn it all seemed pointless.

"Well, I think you'll live, son," Dr. Peters smiled. "Some working over they gave you."

"Yeah!" Glen nodded bitterly, wondering if there was any way possible to ever possess Lynn, marry her, and be her. It all seemed so hopeless.

"When can I get the hell out of here?"

He desperately wanted to see Lynn, hold her dear form in his arms.

"How soon can I split this place?"

"I don't know. Depends on you. You should stay here for a couple of days at least for a rest." The doctor's lined face grew serious. "You want to tell me about this? We could—should, perhaps—call the police."

"Personal!" Glen explained, having decided to remain silent about the details. "I have things I have to tend to and—"

"Stand and try walking," the doctor said. "I know you have nervous feet—at least that's what your friends said." Glen stood, then swayed slightly. His nervous system seemed shaky, but with effort he managed to keep his balance.

The doctor smiled. "See what I mean? Maybe you'd better stay a little while."

Glen shook his head. "Not if I don't have to."

The doctor shrugged: "I can't force you to stay."

The nurse came in just then, said: "There's a call for you, Mr. Fletcher. From a Mrs. Bennings. Do you want to take it?"

Glen jerked straight. *Lynn? The woman must be mistaken.*

He nodded. "Where can I get it?"

"Nurse," the doctor said, "switch the call in here." He turned to Glen. "Want to talk privately?"

"Yes, I think so."

The doctor left the room and a moment later the phone rang on the small table against the wall.

Shaking, Glen picked up the receiver. "Lynn?"

There was a short silence and then a more mature voice said: "No, this is Mrs. Bennings." Hesitation, then: "Are you really serious about this thing between you and Lynn?"

Glen didn't answer for a moment. He was trying to make up his mind about the situation What did Mrs. Bennings want?

"I'm very serious about Lynn," he finally told the woman.

Silence, then haltingly she began talking. "I can arrange it so you two could get together. If you moved fast, you might be able to get away and find some kind of life for yourselves. I only want Lynn to have what she wants. Nothing more! Can you leave the hospital?"

"Yes."

"Okay, then. Tonight, at midnight, have your car parked just down the street from the roadway to the house. Park so that you can see any movement, anybody walking or riding or running down the driveway. Drive up, and immediately open the door, and let Lynn in. She's being held, I'm somewhat afraid, against her will. Earl is planning to take us all on a trip to Europe. He plans on leaving tomorrow. You'll have to move fast. If he finds out what's happening, there's no telling what he'll do! You understand?" Her voice sounded frightened.

"Yes," Glen told her.

"And another thing—if you screw this thing up, Mr. Fletcher, I don't think I would mind putting a hole in your head. I love my daughter, and I don't want to see her hurt unnecessarily, and—"

"You don't have anything to worry about. I love Lynn. I know it's been fast, but things sometimes work out like that, Mrs. Bennings, and—"

"Thanks, Glen. And another thing—if I don't see you, and things work out—good luck and be happy."

She suddenly hung up and he was alone.

MIDNIGHT LOVERS, BY CHARLES NUETZEL

Chapter Fifteen

Glen had parked his car just within sight of the driveway that led up to the distant Bennings' home. It was dark out, so dark that the shadows seemed to have life in their blackness, moving against the night breeze like ghosts from the black side of death.

There had been a fight with Ivy and Hal, who had wanted him to stay in the hospital. He could understand their concern. But to Glen this was something more important than his personal safety, or his career. For the first time in his life he felt that something was more important than trumpet playing. He didn't fool himself; he'd never be able to be completely happy without blowing jazz, but he would never be as happy without Lynn. She had happened so fast, so suddenly in his life, that he still felt slightly dazed over it all. Yet he held no doubts about his feelings.

He waited for a long time before taking out a cigarette and lighting it. His hands were shaking and the soreness around his lips hurt as he dragged on the cigarette.

Glen kept his eyes on the roadway that cut into the highway on which he was parked.

No movement.

He looked at his wrist watch. It was a little after twelve. Mrs. Bennings had said twelve, but that didn't mean that she would be able to get Lynn to his car at the appointed hour. Something could have gone wrong to hold the women up. But what?

He nervously put out the cigarette and then lit another without thinking. Annoyed, he looked at the cigarette and then shrugged, sighed and took a deep, long drag. He could use a drink—a long stiff drink.

His watch said 12:30.

What was taking so long?

Suddenly out of the corner of his eye he saw movement.

Glen jerked to attention, his head turned. Then he saw her. His heart leaped wildly.

Lynn rushed through some bushes, toward the car, and then suddenly was at the door. As he opened the door for her he felt a thrill wave through him.

She slipped into the car without a word, but the look in her eyes said enough to frighten him.

He started the car immediately and gunned the gas. They shot down the road at top speed.

When they'd gotten about two blocks away, Lynn said: "Have a cigarette?"

Her voice was shaky and there was a thick edge of emotion in it that suddenly frightened Glen.

"What's wrong?" he asked.

"I just made it out..." she told him, taking the pack of cigarettes he offered her. A moment later she added, "I'm frightened, Glen. Dad...I've never seen him like this. You should have heard what went on!"

There was a short silence and then she continued. "Mother got the out of the room, and I was just starting through the front hallway when Dad suddenly came out of his study. Oh, God, you don't know what a scare that was! But you haven't heard the last big bit. Mother told me to run—get out of there! Dad must have been too stunned to say anything, or do anything, at first. Then just as I was opening the front door he screamed something—I couldn't make out what it was—but, oh Glen! If Mother hadn't helped—she stopped him for a moment—I guess long enough to get me to your car. What do we do now?"

"Drive like hell for the state line. And hope for the best." Then he cursed. "Hell, why should we have to be running like this? What right does he have to attempt to stop us? You're over twenty-one, and—"

"And Dad has a lot of political pull—in this state, at least. He could make it pretty hard—you dear—what he did to you—I never knew—never thought it was possible for anybody—especially my own father—to do such a thing! I don't know what's wrong with him!" They were silent for a long time.

Then Glen said: "Maybe you're just making more out of this than it really is..."

"You know that's silly, Glen!" Lynn told him. "Dad—well, I always knew that the people in town were frightened to death of him and—well, I just didn't realize what kind of man he could really be."

She sounded frightened.

Just then the sound of a siren came out of the night from behind them.

Lynn grabbed hold of his arm.

"Faster!" she said between tense lips. "Dad's— the cops will do anything he says and..."

Glen gunned the car, speeding down the darkened highway at ninety miles an hour. The car vibrated and the sound of the police siren continued behind them, seeming to get louder and louder.

Glen couldn't help wondering how they had managed to get into such a damned mess, how it could be possible for them to get out of it. The state line was well over thirty miles away and it was impossible to outrun the police for that long, considering they could set up road blocks if Bennings had enough pull to get such an order.

A sinking feeling settled over Glen and he could see himself in a matter of minutes caught in a police trap. The very fantastic element of the situation made it unbelievable, made it possible for him to continue racing down the road to a destiny he had no way of knowing.

* * * * * * *

Earl Bennings stood by the phone, waiting, smoking nervously. He glared at his wife, feeling an angry emotion that he would never have thought possible.

"Goddamn, Mercedes—what the hell right do you have to interfere?" he blurted out for the tenth time.

Mercedes was sitting across the living room from him, staring at her hands, dejected, almost red-faced.

"She has a right to—"

"She has no rights! No rights to ruin her life on

142

some Goddamned slob musician! Believe me—you don't know what you've gotten into!" He hammered his fist against the phone stand and clenched his teeth hard.

Why couldn't they all understand him? Why couldn't they understand he loved Lynn and was looking out for her best interests? All he wanted was for his little girl to be happy! He wanted her to have a good life, the kind he had worked all his life to see that his family got. Now, now that this no good trumpet player had gotten into the picture, all his plans for Lynn were being shot to hell! He had thought to someday see her married to a well to-do man, a man of position and place in the world Not a bum musician who would play around with any girl, who would leave her alone at night to worry and wonder what he was doing—what girl he was laying that night.

Earl Bennings was sick inside; so sick that he couldn't really even let out the pent-up seething anger. For the first time in his life he had come close to deadly violence toward Mercedes and that had scared him. He had felt an insane urge bubbling up in him when Mercedes stopped his charge after Lynn. The moment his daughter had left the house Earl had called the police and told Captain Winters what happened and that he wanted the two brought back, under guard, to his home. Winters, damn him, had given an argument; but Earl had the pull, in the right places, and that had snapped the man into line. A word in the right quarter and Winters wouldn't be Captain Winters any more.

Suddenly the phone rang.

With shaking hands Earl Bennings picked up the

receiver. "Yes?"

"Winters...one of our patrol cars spotted your man. They're giving us a good chase, but we'll put up the road block—if that's what you really want." The voice was hesitant, unsure of itself.

"Damn it, man! Get the block up, and now! I want them back—fast!"

"Don't you think it would be better to..."

"Do as I say. Winters, or you're finished!" Earl Bennings snapped.

"You can't hold an adult without solid charges and—"

"And I'm not holding any adult. That's my daughter. And as far as I'm concerned this...this Fletcher is nothing more than a slick kidnapper! He took advantage of Lynn's inexperience. He wants her money—that's all! I want him stopped before it's too late. Now set the road block up! And fast!" Bennings slammed the receiver on the hook, screamed at the four walls. "Goddamned people! Don't they understand I mean business?"

He picked up the receiver, dialed. Waited. Then, when a sleepy voice answered, he cried:

"Jud—get the hell out here to the house, now!"

"Earl? What's wrong?"

"Lynn's been kidnapped. I want you around!"

There was a long pause and then Jud Renton, Bennings' lawyer, said in a calm tone, "Everything will be all right, Earl. Just calm down and tell me what happened."

"That damned trumpet player took my daughter away from me and they're being picked up by the police. They'll be back here within the hour, and I want you here to...you know what! Put the legal

144

pressure on this man. I want him to understand that I mean business and—"

"Okay...okay...you can tell me all about it when I get there," Jud said in a tired, defeated voice, as if he knew it was no use to argue.

"And fast!" Earl hung up, turned to his wife and said, "You're about to get a sharp lesson on how things really stand. Nobody crosses me! Nobody takes my daughter away. Nobody tries to run my life—or any person around me whom I love! I won't have my daughter marrying a no good and—"

"Please, Earl," Mercedes said, standing,. looking at him. "You're just going to make a damned fool of yourself. There's nothing you can do!"

Earl Bennings laughed, then shook his head. "That's what you think, dear. That's what you think!"

* * * * * * *

Glen didn't feel any real sense of depression at seeing the road block up ahead of them. In fact, he almost felt a sense of relief. This running away, sneaking out, seemed a little too far out!

Automatically he slowed the car, turned for a moment, looked at Lynn and said: "We might as well admit it—this has to be fought out in the open. Your father isn't about to give in that easy. But he's about to meet his match!"

Lynn shook her head slowly from side to side. "You don't know him!"

"You don't know me!" Glen announced tight-lipped as he brought the car to a stop in front of the road block.

Police surged around the car, seeming to come out of the darkness.

"Let's see your driver's..." one of the cops started to say as he looked into the car.

"No need. If you're looking for Glen Fletcher... that's me!" Glen offered.

The police officer frowned and then stood straight, turned and looked at his fellow officers who were not gathered around the driver's seat. "This is the one."

"What now, officer?" Glen asked.

The officer turned again, stared at him, said:

"No trouble?"

"No use," Glen pointed out.

"Okay. Turn the car around, and wait. We'll lead and follow you...to the girl's home." There was a hint of sympathy in the man's voice, as if he were on Glen's side.

"Thanks," Glen told the man, relief bathing over him. At least they had made one point—for what it was worth. Somebody understood their viewpoint; a lot of good it would do them.

He pulled the car around and waited until a police car moved up in front of him. Then as the car started down the road, Glen followed. He glanced at Lynn who was sitting next to him, grim-faced, tight-lipped. Her eyes were moist, and her hand shook as she took a deep drag on her cigarette.

"It'll be all right. There's such a thing as the law. And regardless of what your father thinks he can or can't do, this is the United States of America. He can't change that no matter how much he might want to!" Glen told her, trying to convince himself as well as the woman next to him, of the truth of his

146

statement. What was unnerving was that the police jumped at Bennings' call, even while they apparently didn't agree with him.

MIDNIGHT LOVERS, BY CHARLES NUETZEL

Chapter Sixteen

The long drive back was an awkward study in silence for both of them. Glen found his thoughts running over his past life, and then meeting with the events of the last fantastic days. It had happened so damned fast between Lynn and himself. If the last events hadn't taken place he might not have been quite so sure of himself as he was now. Normally when a whirlwind romance took place it was almost impossible to keep from doubting the rightness of the romance. But Earl Bennings had actually done him a favor. He knew more certainly than ever before that he loved Lynn and would have her regardless of what the cost. Even blowing music seemed distant now. And for the first time in his life he realized a truth that had guided mankind for as long as man had been on the face of the world. Love was the only thing that counted; there just really wasn't anything else. All else was, in fact, mere escaping from loneliness, frustration, confusion. Without love, there was mere emptiness and insanity. He understood his feeling toward women like Ivy, and all the other women he'd known in the past, all the more completely from his experience of the last days, and especially of the last hour. They had been running around chasing their own tails, attempting to find meaning where there was no meaning.

Finally the police car ahead of them turned up the roadway leading to the Bennings' large two-story home. He followed and a few moments later came to a stop in front of the other car.

Turning, he faced Lynn. "Look, dear, this is going to be tough. I can only imagine how tough it will be for you. All I know is that I love you. I don't give a damn about anything else. No matter what your father has to say or tries to do, it won't mean anything to me or how I feel about you! Do you understand that?"

Lynn nodded and then suddenly flung herself into his arms.

"I love you so much, Glen!" she cried, hugging tightly to him.

"I love you, too." Then after a moment he added, "Maybe it's better this way. Maybe it'll be better for all concerned. Now he'll have to face the fact that we love each other—that we want to get married—and no matter how much he screams, it won't do him a damned bit of good!"

The door opened on Lynn's side of the car and a police officer was politely waiting for them.

Slowly breaking out of the embrace, Glen touched his lips against Lynn's forehead and said, "Chin up—and don't let down an inch!"

He opened the door at his side as the officer helped Lynn out of the car. They were flanked by officers as they went up to the large porch. The front door burst open and Earl Bennings stood there like some avenging devil from hell itself. His eyes blazed fire and hate toward Glen and only softened

150

when they turned to his daughter.

"You're all right?" he cried in an emotional voice, reaching out his arms toward Lynn.

Lynn ignored her father, said coldly, "What'd you expect? That I'd be raped by the man I love— and the man who loves me?"

She brushed past Earl Bennings without another word, without even looking at the man. Glen felt a wave of satisfaction and pity as he saw the hurt expression on Bennings' heavy features as he stepped into the house behind Lynn.

They were ushered into the drawing room in which waited a police captain and a thin, bald, nervous man with a line moustache on his large upper lip.

Mercedes Bennings rushed toward her daughter and embraced her. "Oh, I hoped that you'd..."

"It's all right, Mother," Lynn told the older woman. Then after a quick hug, Lynn turned and stepped to Glen's side, took hold of his hand and squeezed it. Her fingers were damp and shaky.

Earl Bennings stood in the middle of the room, glaring at Glen. For a long time he didn't say anything. The air seemed to weigh down on the room like a blanket so thick and solid it would have seemed possible to cut it in pieces.

Glen took the silence as a good chance to take the lead.

"Look, Mr. Bennings, I don't know what you have in mind, but this is all really just a lot of unnecessary physical and verbal abuse! You can't hold Lynn against her will...and that's exactly what you're doing!"

Bennings snapped tense, like a jungle tiger. He

151

leaped across the room and thrust his large face at Glen.

"Damn you, don't tell me my rights, you punk!" His hands doubled up into fists, and for a moment it looked as if he were about to hit Glen. Then a slow, even grin spread across his face.

"Almost got to me, son," he said silkily.

Bennings turned to the nervous looking man with the moustache. "You tell this...man, Jud!"

Jud Renton stepped forward, his face blank of emotion, his eyes veiled. When he spoke his voice was assured, careful, in complete control.

"Young man, I think it would be advisable that you back out of this thing before it gets you in too deep. Mr. Bennings is willing to be very generous. Believe me, very generous! It will be made well worth your while! You name the figure, and he'll make out a check. If you don't—well, you can see how things are!"

Glen stood there, stunned, unable to believe the coldness in the man's words. Right in front of Lynn. How could Bennings possibly do such a thing?

"Okay," Glen countered, smiling. "I'll tell you what. I have a price—but it will cost. It'll be much higher than Mr. Bennings is willing to pay!"

Earl Bennings' face brightened, his eyes snapped to his daughter with an expression that said: *I told you so!*

Jud said: "I wouldn't try being smart, Mr. Fletcher. While Bennings is willing to give you anything you want, it would be very foolish of you to."

"Just stow it!" Glen said angrily. He squeezed Lynn's hand. He had felt the woman tense almost to stone when he'd made his answer to Jud.

152

Glen looked at Bennings. "The price is quite simple. You can take your money and stuff it! I don't want a damned dime! Ever! And you aren't about to give your daughter a damned dime! The full price is your daughter. And the moment you tell your paid-off police to let us go, we'll leave!"

There was a long stunned silence in the room. Glen's eyes flashed around to the different people standing around them. There were several reactions showing.

Mercedes was beaming happily. The police captain's face had hardened to rigid steel. Jud Renton had merely put a harder veil over his features; it was impossible to tell what he was thinking.

The police captain was the first to speak. He glared at Glen. "I don't like your remark! The implication is—"

"Quite true. What charges did you have us brought in on? Name them."

The captain looked confused for a moment and then he turned to Jud as if looking for legal advice.

Bennings said: "Tell them, Jud. That's what you're here for! You're the *great* lawyer. Now do something to earn your pay!"

Jud, for the first time, looked ill at ease. "Young man, do you know that it is illegal to have relations with an unmarried young woman in this state? That you can go to jail for a long, long time?"

"And who is this woman?" Glen asked.

Jud snapped back. "There was that singer of yours—and—"

"And you can't prove a thing!" Glen countered. "You're bluffing, and you know it! You have to have a complaint! Go and get one, if you think you can! Then we can talk about such a trumped up charge!"

Bennings grinned, his eyes turning to the police captain. "I can have you arrested—held long enough so that I can take my daughter out of the country, where you can't reach her. How would you be then? Why don't you be sensible?"

Glen felt an icy hand run across his spine. He looked at Jud. "Okay, let's all be sensible. I'm in favor of that."

"Okay," Jud agreed.

"Why don't we let the main person involved say how she feels about this?" Glen's eyes snapped to the police captain and then back to the lawyer.

Silence answered him, until Bennings cried:

"She's just a child! That's the whole point. I'm trying to save her from this money grubber! This tramp! That—"

Jud cut in with, "Earl, keep out of this!"

For a stunned moment Bennings stood there with his mouth open, then he snapped his lips shut.

Jud turned to Lynn. "You know the situation better than anybody else here, Lynn. You know your father could have this man arrested, held long enough to...well, to make things difficult for you, and—"

"Jud," Lynn cut in, "don't you honestly think this is really just a big farce? Dad can't do a thing...and you all know it. You're all bluffing. You're all just trying to make Glen look like a young fortune hunter. You aren't getting anywhere. You know that my father can't take me anywhere against my will, any more than Glen can. If you put Glen in jail, I'll make sure that Dad can't take me

154

out of the city! If I have to break every law, you'll have to put me in jail—and *keep* me there! Now, put that in your pipes and smoke it!" Her grin challenged them.

Silence followed and then slowly Jud turned and faced Bennings. "Earl, I can't help doing this, but I'll have to advise you on the truth of the situation. You really don't have any legal grounds. I tried to tell you that from the beginning, but you wouldn't listen. Lynn is old enough to do what she wants and—"

"She's just a child! She doesn't have the right to ruin her life and—"

"Every adult has the right to do with their life what they want. That's the whole point of the law. When a person turns twenty-one they have the right to make their own mistakes. You can't take that away from them. Sure, you could have this man arrested on a lot of trumped up charges, but you would only be holding off what will happen in any event—either with this man, or somebody else. You can't take charge of an adult and try to run their lives against their will. He really seems to love your daughter. That's better than taking a chance on somebody else. I've looked into him...a little...and he seems to be an up and coming musician. And musicians today are different from what they used to be when you ran speakeasies! The facts are you are in the wrong here. No matter how it hurts: You can pull strings—and we'll all jump to your smallest wish, because we all owe you something—but you can't change the law. In the end you'll lose your daughter completely. Why don't you realize that there are some people you can't run!"

Jud's shoulders sagged after his little speech, as if he were afraid he'd gone too far, but hadn't been able to keep from saying what he had said.

Bennings looked at the floor for some time and then finally turned his eyes toward Lynn. He started to say something and then turned his attention to Glen.

"Why...why are you doing this to me?" Bennings cried. "What did I do to you—" He broke off, as if realizing how foolish his words sounded.

Glen suddenly felt sorry for Bennings. He said:

"I love your daughter. I love her very much... and I'm not the kind of guy who falls that easy— even if it happened that fast. Sometimes it happens like that. Actually you've given me a chance to prove to you, to Lynn—and maybe even to myself—just how much I do love her. We'd much rather be on speaking terms with you—but that's up to you!"

Glen put his arm around Lynn and hugged her warmly.

Bennings' face slowly softened. He looked at Mercedes, as if pleading for support.

His wife stepped forward to his side and said:

"Earl, we both love Lynn. I understand more than you know...why you, well, acted like this. Why don't we clear away all these other people and have a talk with the kids before they run off and get married?"

Bennings looked at his daughter one more time and then nodded. He merely said to the others:

"Could you leave us? I'm sorry."

* * * * * * *

It was the next morning; a long night stretched out behind them. But strangely it all seemed a wonderful night, considering how things had worked out.

As Glen got into his car next to Lynn he smiled, pressed her hand with his, then turned and looked at Earl Bennings who was standing outside on his side of the car.

Bennings said, "You're a fighter. I'm glad Mercedes told you about...what happened years before. I guess we understand each other, at least a little better." The man reached out and touched Glen's shoulder.

"At least I have a fighter as a son-in-law!" he grinned.

Glen felt a wave of compassion for the older man. It hadn't been easy for Earl Bennings to tell him about the affair that his wife had had with another musician many years before. Bennings had taken Glen into his private study to tell him.

It was a private matter just between the two of them. If Lynn's mother had said anything to Lynn, Glen didn't know. Maybe someday they would discover they both had been told. Hate could do a lot of weird things to a person. Maybc in the future Earl Bennings would be a little more understanding toward his wife; toward other people. Glen hoped so.

He started the car, waved good-bye to Mercedes, who was on Lynn's side, and then gently pressed the gas pedal. Not until they were on the main highway did either of them say anything.

Lynn broke the silence. "Did Dad tell you about Mom and the—"

"Your mother told you, too?"

Lynn nodded. "I'm sorry for them."

"You shouldn't be, Lynn. At least they did manage to stay together. Maybe that's the important thing."

"I didn't mean that, Glen. It's just that...well, with all their money, how much happiness do you think Dad has? I never realized it before, but I think he lived too much...for me."

"Well, he's learned you can't live somebody else's life for them," Glen pointed out.

They were quiet for some time, then Glen asked: "How do you like being Mrs. Fletcher?"

She squeezed his arm. "At least sometimes it pays to have a father with political pull," she laughed.

Glen grinned, thinking about how fast things had moved. Once Bennings had realized how completely defeated he was and all of them had come to an understanding, the older man had made a few calls and an hour later a marriage ceremony had taken place in the Bennings' living room. It had been a quiet affair, with only Lynn's parents as witnesses. Glen was happy that it had turned out that way.

"Where now?" Lynn asked in a small voice.

"Honeymoon time—then to Vegas, and I guess that'll seem like another honeymoon, to you. Then I'm going to arrange things so that we work at one location. We can settle down in a large house and raise a lot of children and—"

"And you'll do nothing of the sort, Mr. Glen Fletcher!" Lynn told him in a stern voice. "You'll just work all the harder to make yourself that big

158

name! And we'll talk about homes at a future date. After all, you don't think I married you because you're the most handsome man in the world, or because I loved you, did you?"

"Well, I had hoped that was the reason," Glen told her, grinning.

"Isn't that like a man! A big ego, I married you because of the glamour! Just think, visiting all those cities...You can do that much for me—for a while, at least. Then we can settle down a little—after you're on top!" She was thoughtful for a moment, then asked: "That won't be too long, will it?"

Glen laughed happily. "It shouldn't be too long, no."

In fact, Glen realized, it shouldn't be long at all, since he was already blowing at top prices. There wasn't any reason in the world he couldn't settle down in Los Angeles, work as a studio musician, do recordings, have a few gigs with a group throughout Los Angeles and Vegas in order to keep in the public eye. But all that wasn't really important to him any more. The most important thing in life was sitting next to him: Lynn Fletcher. And nothing else really mattered. As long as he could make her happy, he would be the happiest man alive!

About the Author

Charles Nuetzel was born in San Francisco in 1934, and writes:

"As long as I can remember I wanted to be a writer. It was a dream I never thought would materialize. But with the help of Forrest J Ackerman, who became my agent, I managed to finally make it into print.

"I was lucky enough not only in selling my work to publishers but also ending up packaging books for some of them, and finally becoming a 'publisher' much like those who had bought my first novels. From there it as a simple leap to editing not only a sci-fi anthology, but a line of sci-fi books for Powell Sci-Fi back in the 1960s. Throughout these active professional years I had the chance to design some covers and do graphic cover layouts for pocket books & magazines."

Much of his work in covers and graphics are a result of having had a father who was a professional commercial artist, and who did a number of covers for sci-fi magazines in the 1950s and later for pocket books—even for some of Mr. Nuetzel's books.

In retirement he has become involved in swing dancing, a long time lover of Big Band jazz. But more interestingly world travels have taken him (and his wife Brigitte) across the world, to Hawaii, Caribbean, Mexico, Kenya, Egypt, Peru, having a lifelong interest in ancient civilizations. His website is full of thousands of pictures taken during these trips.